"You goin' home on t... ...
to sound casual, to get u... ...
having to make a big dea... ...

Lance didn't even loo... ...
a ride," he said, and started to walk off.

"Randy!" I burst out, forgetting to be casual. "What is this with you and Randy hanging out together? Randy's a jerk."

Lance threw me one backward glance as he walked away. "Randy's a cool guy," he said. "He doesn't mess around with other people's lives."

Yeah, great. Randy doesn't mess around with other people's lives, but I do, right? Just that once I'd got involved where I didn't belong and it looked like Lance was going to hold it against me forever.

Marilyn Halvorson lives in Alberta, Canada. She runs her own cattle ranch where she also raises and trains horses. She has written stories about life in the West since she was given a typewriter for Christmas when she was twelve.

Besides ranching, and writing, Marilyn Halvorson teaches Junior High School. She has done this for fifteen years and says that she gets many of her writing ideas from her students. She understands young people and thinks this may be because "I was often a thoroughly miserable teenager. I always felt like I wasn't making it at fitting in as one of the gang."

Not surprisingly, her stories are enormously popular. *Let It Go* was so successful when first published that she wrote a sequel, *Nobody Said It Would Be Easy*.

Let It Go

Marilyn Halvorson

Let It Go

ARMADA

Let It Go was first published in Canada in 1985
by Irwin Publishing Inc. and first published in
the UK in Armada in 1989

Armada is an imprint of
the Children's Division, part of
the Collins Publishing Group,
8 Grafton Street, London W1X 3LA

Copyright © 1985 Marilyn Halvorson

Printed and bound in Great Britain by
William Collins Sons & Co. Ltd, Glasgow

*To the kids who were in my split
grades five and six classes.
Thanks for two very special years.
And to all the friends who take the time
to listen, and listen, and listen . . .*

1

First period Friday morning we get math. Math is always bad but today was worse. We were reviewing some meaningless misery called Motion Geometry. Don't ask me why they call it that. Probably because you could get motion sickness doing all those flips and slides with those stupid little shapes.

Just when I was afraid I was about to enter the Guinness Book of Records as the first person in history to actually die of boredom, the intercom cut in. I sighed with relief. Any interruption gratefully accepted!

"Excuse me, Mrs. Jackson." The secretary's voice sounded metallic over the PA system. "Would you please send Jared Cantrell and Lance Ducharme to the office immediately."

Almost any interruption. This one made my stomach do a flip and slide that beat anything that math book had to offer. Still, I wasn't really surprised that Mr. Schafer had found out. We should have known we'd never get away with it. But it had seemed like a good idea at the time.

Lance and I exchanged glances and Mrs. Jackson gave us a kind of tired, "not-again" look and nodded toward the door. We walked out of the room, acting cool and unconcerned, like movie heroes who are about to die. It seemed like we'd had a lot of practice at that lately.

Out in the hall, I gave Lance a dirty look. "You and your big ideas," I muttered.

He grinned and shrugged. "Gee, I didn't think anybody'd miss us. We must be pretty popular, huh?"

That was Lance for you. Here I was, having a heart attack, and he thought the whole thing was funny. It was always like that with him — nothing worried him and it seemed like he could get away with anything.

We walked into the main office and just sort of stood around until Mrs. Kreswell, the secretary, finally noticed us. "Oh, it's you two again," she said, trying to sound stern but not quite making it. Usually, we got along real good with Mrs. Kreswell — except for one time when we had to wait a long time in the office so, for something to do, while she was busy at the filing cabinet, we took all the paper clips out of the box on her desk, made them into a chain, and put them back in the box. There were 456 of them. I counted. They made a real long chain. She was kind of grumpy after that for awhile. I don't know why.

Now, she nodded to the scarred wooden bench along the wall. "You'll have to wait a while," she said.

The bench was familiar territory. We had spent some time there in the past couple of years. To tell the truth, quite a lot of time. In fact, if they ever start selling reserved seats for waiting to see the principal, they'll probably want Lance and me to buy season tickets.

We sat down. Never, in all my numerous visits to Mr. Schafer, has he ever been ready to see me when I get there. I think the waiting is part of the punishment. I can just about hear some professor in university lecturing while all these future principals take notes. "And above all, remember to keep them waiting a long time. That softens up the little savages like nothing else." And, in my case, he would be dead right. I can't wait more than five minutes for anything before I start getting restless — and when I'm waiting to find out how much trouble I'm in I can beat a long-tailed cat in a roomful of rocking chairs at being restless.

I shifted around, trying to get comfortable. Lance looked at me. "You gettin' nervous?" he asked.

"No," I lied, and then added, "But my sunburn is killin' me." And that sure wasn't a lie. It got real hot yesterday afternoon while we were studying extra-curricular fishing so we took our shirts off to get a tan. One of Lance's typically dumb ideas. He needs a tan like a turtle needs running shoes and I couldn't get a decent tan if you put me in the microwave. You see, Lance is about half Cree and, even in the middle of an Alberta January, he looks like he just walked off the beach at San Diego. But I've got red hair — and give me an hour in the sun and I'll have the skin to match. I've seen boiled lobsters that looked better.

I could see that Lance was getting ready with a smart remark but, fortunately, he didn't get the chance. Mrs. Kreswell's intercom phone rang and after she listened a minute she said, "All right, I'll send them in."

I took a deep breath and heard Lance do the same. Slowly, we stood up and walked toward the principal's closed door. Mrs. Kreswell stopped us. "Unh-unh, Mr. Schafer's away at a meeting. Miss Cassidy wants to see you this time."

Lance looked at me. "Do you think that's good news or bad news?" he asked in a low voice.

"It depends," I muttered. "It just depends." I was

probably one of the few people who had ever seen Cassidy really mad. And I sure didn't want to see it again.

I knocked on the door marked "Guidance Counsellor".

"Come in." Cassidy's voice wasn't giving away any clues to her disposition today. We stepped inside. She was sitting behind her desk. At least, I guess there was a desk there, somewhere. Cassidy's desk has the same reputation as the Bermuda Triangle. Whatever goes there is lost forever, buried in piles of papers, books, three-year-old memos — you name it, she's got it. Just don't expect her to be able to find it.

"Close the door, Jared," she said. Jared? I thought. She'd been calling me Red ever since she was my homeroom teacher, two years ago. This was going to be one heavy interview. I closed the door.

"Sit down, Jared. You, too, Lance." We sat. And she sat. Looking at us and waiting long enough for the silence to get louder than a shotgun blast. My sunburn started itching again but I didn't dare even twitch. I tried to read Cassidy's expression but, as usual, I couldn't. She could be really inscrutable sometimes.

There was probably one — and only one — advantage to being sent to Mr. Schafer instead of Cassidy. Mr. Schafer was as predictable as a re-run. You knew he would yell at you and pound on his desk and, if you'd really made him mad, he might give you a few whacks with the Board of Education.

But with Cassidy you never knew. It was sort of exciting.

At last, she broke the silence. "Are you feeling better, Jared?" she asked, her face real serious.

Feeling better? I'd been ready for almost anything except a chat about my health. I looked at Lance, hoping he could give me some clue as to what I might have been sick with. But, he was studying the floor like he'd never seen one before. No help at all.

"Yeah, well, I mean, no . . . I'm not . . ." I stumbled around until I finally decided to shut up long enough to take my foot out of my mouth.

Cassidy raised her eyebrows. "You mean that yesterday afternoon's sudden absence wasn't the result of an attack of Bubonic Plague or something equally interesting?"

I had a feeling that it was one of those questions you weren't actually supposed to answer.

She shifted her attack. "And you, Lance? Were you sick yesterday afternoon?"

There was a long silence and I half-expected him to come up with one of his famous lines. I'll never forget when he came back last spring after being away for a day and Cassidy asked him where he'd been. "Oh, I had to go to the eye doctor," he'd answered, real seriously. She was ready to swallow that as being perfectly normal. "Yeah, and while I was there I fell into the lens-grinding machine and made a terrible spectacle of myself."

Well, the whole class had broken up over that and nobody had laughed louder than Cassidy. But, even if he can con teachers into almost anything, Lance is a lousy liar. Now, he looked up and, "No, ma'am," was all he said.

Cassidy nodded. "I see," she said slowly. "Well, this does present an interesting problem. If you two weren't sick and, obviously, you weren't at school —" she paused long enough to let that fact sink in, then leaned forward, and gave us a long, level look. "Where exactly *were* you?"

When it comes right down to it, I'm a lousy liar, too. Anyhow, if I made up some complicated story, she'd probably phone home to check it out. And that kind of trouble I didn't need.

I looked up. "Fishin'," I said.

"Fishin'," she repeated solemnly.

Lance and I nodded.

"You skipped Career Fair to go fishing?"

We nodded again. It was the terrible truth. We had passed up an afternoon of wandering through a dozen classrooms, listening to a bunch of boring people drone on about the wonders of being everything from plumbers to orthodontists. I'd been through it all last year and if that was all the future had to offer I'd decided I might as well stay in school until I was old enough to retire.

"Why did you skip out, Red?" she asked, more curiously than angrily, and since she was calling me Red, things seemed to be looking up considerably.

"Well," I said, trying to find the right words, "Career Fair is about as exciting as sitting around watching the dust settle."

She almost smiled, but got herself under control and looking inscrutable again. "I see. And were they biting?"

"Who?" I asked, half-startled. My mind had been on the buck-toothed orthodontist at the Fair last year.

"The fish, of course. Did you catch any?"

I shook my head.

"Well, I'm not surprised. The only thing that will catch trout in May is dew worms. You should try them."

Wow. This was turning into a pretty weird visit. We come in here to get punished for skipping and end up getting hot tips on trout fishing. Unfortunately, Cassidy wasn't quite finished. She chewed her pencil thoughtfully and said, "Now, what am I going to do about you two?"

Give us a weekend assignment to practise your fishing advice? I almost asked. But you just don't want to push your luck with Cassidy.

Then, her eyes came to rest on a memo on her desk. It was from the janitor and it must have just arrived. It was only half buried. "The bathroom poet has been at work," she read aloud, with a puzzled look on her face. Then, she nodded. "Oh yes, the graffiti again. And definitely lacking in delicacy," she added in an irritated tone. Suddenly, she looked at us and her face lit up. "I have just the job for you boys," she said brightly. "After school, get some cleaning equipment from the janitor and scrub down the walls of the boys' bathroom. It shouldn't take more than an hour or two, and since you missed three hours of school yesterday . . ."

Lance and I looked at each other. When you've been set up with that much style you might just as well keep quiet.

"Okay, you can go now," Cassidy said. "Have a good day." We were halfway out the door when she stopped me. "Oh, by the way, Red. Next time you decide to sneak off inconspicuously, put a bag over your head. That's the only way you're ever going to get that hair of yours out the back door unrecognized." She grinned and closed the door behind us before I could think of anything to say — which was probably just as well. Anything I could have thought of to say would have got me into a whole new bunch of trouble.

"Very funny," I muttered. Then I turned to look at Lance. He was laughing. "Aw, shut up," I growled and took a half-hearted swing at him. He ducked and we both detoured into the bathroom to kill the last few minutes of math class and study our future employment.

As I walked past the mirror I caught a glimpse of my reflection and that just made me madder. Cassidy was right. That stupid red hair was as bad as wearing a name tag. Only three people in the whole school had hair that colour — and the other two were girls.

We checked out the walls. They were pretty well

graffitied, all right; though most of it definitely did lack delicacy, a few of them were pretty funny. We were going to be scrubbing for a long time.

Everybody in our class knew we had cut school yesterday afternoon so they were fairly sure we hadn't been called to the office to receive good conduct awards. Naturally, they were all dying of curiosity about what had happened down there but we played it cool, acting kind of pained and quiet, hoping they'd think that Schafer had beat the heck out of us. That always makes you a hero around school. But, as Lance put it, "Unless they start passing out purple hearts for dishpan hands, nobody gets hero-status for scrubbing the washroom walls."

I had a nasty suspicion that Cassidy might have had that exact thought in mind when she dreamed up this punishment.

"Oh, well," Lance added cheerfully, "maybe if we just act inconspicuous about it, nobody will find out."

"Yeah," I said sourly. "That's what you said about sneaking out yesterday."

He grinned. "So, now we've had more practice."

2

When that three o'clock bell rings, it has the same effect on the school as somebody yelling "Shark!" on a swimming beach. Instant evacuation. And normally Lance and I would have been leading the pack. It took real talent for us to be the last ones to leave without it looking like we had to stay. Of course, the fact that Lance managed to accidentally flip open the rings of his binder while holding it upside-down held us up considerably. Two hundred pages of assorted notes from five subjects drifted to earth like leaves in an October breeze.

Lance groaned, swore under his breath, and kicked his locker. Then, he sank to his knees and started picking up papers. And, naturally, being his best friend and all, I had to stay and help him.

The halls were empty before we half-finished gathering up those papers. Suddenly, a thought hit me. I turned to Lance. "How do you think Cassidy really found out about us skipping? You think somebody ratted on us?"

He shook his head. "No, I think she was telling the truth. She really did recognize us —"

"Yeah, yeah," I interrupted, disgusted. "My hair. My glorious, unmistakeable red hair."

Lance laughed. "Don't take it so hard, Red," he said, reaching out to mess up that same hair. "It looks real good with your glorious, unmistakeable freckles."

Freckles! That did it. I didn't even have freckles — well, maybe one or two. Hair teasing was bad enough, but freckles? No way! I jumped on him and we started wrestling right in the middle of all his notes. By the time Miss Cassidy came along we had pretty well destroyed science and social studies and were putting some serious wrinkles in language arts. She was not impressed. We began work on the washroom walls immediately.

At first, we talked while we scrubbed, but by the time we were half done we'd about run out of interesting conversation. So we just scrubbed. I was going at it for all I was worth, my mind on the fact that this was Friday evening coming up, and that for me it would be wasted. Just like every other Friday for two years now . . . . Another of those Friday night trips with Mom and Dad. I got so mad, and was scrubbing so hard, that water oozed out of the sponge and trickled down my arm.

Suddenly, I got that being-watched feeling. I turned around. Lance had quit working and was leaning against the wall with that big white grin plastered from ear to ear. Grinning and watching me scrub. "Paleface work heap hard," he said. Then he laughed. "Hey, man, you didn't need to go to Career Fair. You've got a great future ahead of you — as a janitor."

"Shut up, Geronimo!" I growled, and sailed my wet sponge at him. He ducked and it smacked the wall above his head. He bent over to pick it up, still with that lazy grin on his face.

Something about the way he looked just then seemed familiar. Suddenly, it struck me. "Hey," I said. "Remember that time I got in the fight with Brian Connelly?"

Lance laughed. "Remember it? That fight was the highlight of the year."

"For you, maybe. You were doing the watchin'. I was doing the bleedin'."

"Yeah, you kinda outclassed yourself that time, didn't you?"

Outclassed was an understatement. Even back then Connelly had stood about five-nine or ten and was built like a heavyweight wrestler. Anybody who got into a fight with him had to be one of two things —a karate champion or an idiot. And, unfortunately, I wasn't into martial arts . . .

But I was the new kid in Alderton. The know-it-all city kid out to make a reputation in this dump of a town. Maybe my dad could drag me out here to the outskirts of the world, but there was no way he could make me fit in here.

That's the way I had felt about moving here, two Septembers ago. There was nothing I was going to like about Alderton, and that included the kids here. In my opinion, they mainly fitted into three groups —the wimps, the hoods, and the wimps who thought they were hoods. I hated all of them. But if I had to have somebody to hang around with, I'd pick the hoods.

Even if I *was* the new cop's kid — no, *especially* because I was the new cop's kid — I was going to show everybody that I could be as tough as any kid in town. It seemed like I got in an average of one fight a week trying to prove that. And I guess the principal figured that since my dad was a cop he'd want to hear about it every time I got in trouble at school. So Dad got dragged down to the school about once a week. Things were not exactly on a friendly basis around our house those days. They aren't much better these days, but that's a long story . . .

"What did you and Connelly ever tangle over, anyhow?" Lance asked, interrupting my thinking.

"Suzie Melton," I sighed. "We both thought we were going steady with her." Actually "going steady" was a pretty strange way to describe it. We really didn't "go" anywhere. The way it worked was, you wrote each other's initials on your binders and, if you were really serious, you sometimes walked out to the bus together. Not exactly an earth-shaking romance. But back then it was hot stuff.

"Suzie moved at the end of term, didn't she?" Lance asked, making a few lazy swipes at the wall with my captured sponge. "I can't even remember what she looked like."

"I can," I said. "She looked like a raccoon with a hangover."

Lance stopped scrubbing. "A what?" he said, looking like he was considering buying a hearing aid.

"Eye make-up," I explained. "Under, over and around. I think she bought it in bulk at a discount store."

Lance laughed. "But you thought she was beautiful enough to die for."

"Yeah," I admitted sheepishly. "And by the time Connelly got done with me I was afraid I might really get the chance to!"

"You were pretty messed up all right."

Messed up wasn't the half of it. Just like it was yesterday, I can still remember that fight.

"Give it to him!" Those were Connelly's buddies, the guys I wanted to get friendly with. Fat chance! Connelly had beat me in about two minutes, but by that time my temper had taken over and every time he knocked me down I got up and came back for more. I was almost out on my feet when I heard a voice that seemed to come from a long way off. "Hey, come on, Connelly, lay off. You've got him beat."

The schoolyard was rotating in big, lazy circles. I could barely see who was doing the talking. Lance

Ducharme. A big, dark, good-looking guy who was in the same class as me. Of all the kids in there he was probably the only one who didn't fit into any of my categories. He seemed to get along okay with all of the groups but he didn't really hang out with any of them or play team sports or any of that stuff. He lived out near us. His dad ran Silverwinds, the biggest ranch around Alderton, and it seemed like Lance always had to be at home helping him instead of hanging around with the other kids. Lance was kind of a cowboy type — a fact that didn't impress me much at the time.

Anyway, while all that was going through my head, the world made one extra-fast circle and the next thing I knew I was on the ground. Then, before I had time to figure out if there was anything I could move that didn't hurt, Ducharme was dragging me to my feet.

"Come on," he said to me in a low voice, "if you don't get outa here before a teacher shows up, Schafer will have your old man in here again."

I didn't understand why he was bothering to get involved but I sure wasn't in any shape to argue. Dazed as I was, though, I noticed that Connelly didn't give Ducharme any trouble about stopping the fight. I'd never seen Ducharme in a fight, but there was something about him that made even the tough guys keep their distance.

"You remember dragging me into the washroom so my dad wouldn't find out about the fight?" I asked curiously.

Lance grinned. "How could I forget? The first thing you did was throw up."

I remembered that part too. All too clearly.

Getting punched in the stomach right after lunch doesn't do much for the digestion. After *that*, I doused my head with cold water and began to have a vague hope I might live. It was then that I remembered Lance. He was standing there, leaning against the wall, just like he was now, and studying me as if he was taking notes on the behaviour of a rat for his biology project.

"Cantrell," he'd said at last, "why don't you quit tryin' so hard?" The way he said it, kind of half-mockingly, like there was a grin just below the surface, didn't go over very well with me. For a minute I wondered if I was up to fighting him, too, but I decided I'd have to settle for giving him a dirty glare — and even that wasn't easy with one eye swollen shut.

"What's that supposed to mean?" I snarled.

The glare didn't seem to have impressed him much. He didn't move and the look on his face didn't change much, except maybe to let a hint of the hidden grin come out. "You know what I mean," he said. "Ever since you moved to Alderton, you've been trying to prove something to somebody. You go around acting so cool you need thermal underwear just to keep from freezing solid, and what's it getting you? Beat up. And for what? To impress all the local punks with how tough you are? Well, they aren't impressed. No matter how hard you try you can't beat them at being rotten. They've been practising longer and they're just naturally better at it. So why don't you skip the big routine and have a shot at just being yourself? Who knows, you might accidentally turn out to be a nice guy." Now he really was grinning, grinning and waiting for me to make the next move.

I didn't say anything for a long time. I didn't see why I had to take that kind of garbage from him — especially since it was almost all true. "You finished?" I muttered, at last.

He nodded. "Yeah, I'm finished." He stood up and

moved away from the wall. "Now, if you're planning on slugging me for saying it, go ahead and get it over with. If you're not, let's go get a Coke from the machine before the bell rings." Then, he'd flashed that startling white grin again. "You're buying. I'm broke."

I had bought the Coke. And we'd been friends ever since.

I came back to the present.

"Hey, give me back my sponge," I said, grinning. "And you owe me a Coke."

3

It was nearly five o'clock when we started walking home. It was only two miles to Lance's place and then another half to mine but I still wasn't looking forward to the walk. Not with thunder rumbling over the hills to the west and the sky turning that threatening blue-black that means it's about to dump a lot of water any minute. Any other time, there would have been half a dozen people we knew drive by and offer us a ride, but today it seemed like everyone must have got there already or else they weren't planning to go. Cars were scarcer than clothes at a nudist convention and it was beginning to look like we were doomed to get wet.

Then, just as the first drops of rain began to fall, a car came up behind us — and it wasn't just any car. *No one* in Alderton owned a car like this.

It was a Lincoln Continental, all silver and black, with customized everything. It practically breathed dollar signs out its exhaust as it came floating up behind us as smooth as those clouds were sailing across the sky. Then, just as it pulled up beside us, it slowed down, and I had a crazy feeling that they were actually going to stop and give us a ride. But the car didn't stop. It just cruised on by, real slow, like the people inside were taking a good look at us. I got a pretty good look at them, too. A man and a woman. He had a black moustache, a white stetson, and "creep" was the first word I would have picked to describe him. I couldn't see the woman as well. Good-looking, young, with a lot of curly, black hair was about all I could make out because she was turned away from me, talking to the man. It looked like they might have been arguing about something. Then they must have settled the argument because, suddenly, the car speeded up and was gone. The last thing I noticed was that it had out-of-province licence plates. I thought I read "Tennessee" but I wasn't sure.

Lance and I looked at each other. "It's the Mafia," he said, very seriously. "Mr. Schafer found out about us skipping yesterday afternoon so he hired them to blow us away."

"Yeah, sure. And since when does the godfather wear a cowboy hat?"

Lance swung around and grabbed me by the jacket collar. "You better listen, kid," he hissed through his teeth, "and you better listen good. I'm tellin' you the godfather wears *whatever* he wants, see?" It was the worst imitation of a 1940's movie hood I'd ever heard. He let go of my jacket. "Well, did I sound like Humphrey Bogart?" he asked, grinning.

I shook my head. "Naw, more like John Travolta."

He thought that over. "You mean Italian and sexy?"

"No, I mean Brooklyn and dumb."

That ended the conversation. It's hard to talk when you're running for your life.

Five minutes later it was really raining and I'd about resigned myself to the fact that we were going to get soaked. Then I heard it. It was way back behind us, probably just at the town limits, but that sound was unmistakeable. A Corvette, growling deep in its throat as it started to accelerate. And there was only one Corvette in town.

Lance had heard it, too. "Here comes good ol' Randy," he said. Sure enough, it was Randy. At first, the car was just a white dot against the black of the wet pavement but it was whistling toward us like a Lear Jet on a runway. Rain, snow, ice, or hail, nothing slowed Randy down. He passed us doing 80 mph, at least; then, he hit the brakes. The back end whipped back and forth across that rain-slick hardtop leaving big rubber S's plastered across it like a sloppy signature.

Oh, great, I thought. He's gonna roll it and guess who'll be around to scrape up what's left of him. A perfect ending for a perfect day.

But, somehow, he managed to stay right-side-up through a screeching skid that ended with the 'vette sitting sideways across the road. He slammed it into reverse and came burning back toward us so fast that, for a second, I thought I was in one of those "Dirty Harry" type movies where the bad guy tries to run down the hero, misses, and comes back for another try.

Randy jammed on the brakes and rocked to a stop beside us. He stuck his head out the window and hollered something, but "Motley Crüe" was blasting from the tape deck at hearing-impairment volume so I could only guess that he was offering us a ride.

I was closest to the car so I supposed it was up to me to answer. Well, in the first place, I didn't like Randy Borowski and I knew that, if it was possible, Lance liked him even less. And, in the second place, if my dad ever caught me in Randy's company, let alone his car, he'd ground me for so long that I'd be ready for the old age pension before I saw the sun again.

On the other hand, it was pouring bucketsful of freezing-cold rain out there and we were still a mile from Lance's place. But that wasn't what really made up my mind for me. It was the car that did it. Don't ask me to pass up a ride in a Corvette. I mean, just don't.

"Sure!" I yelled and ran for the passenger door. I didn't look back but I knew that Lance would be right behind me. However he felt about Randy, he still had enough sense to come in out of the rain.

We piled in on the passenger side and squeezed into the bucket seat. Obviously, Corvettes are designed for people who only have one friend. Maybe that was why Randy drove one. Come to think of it, I wasn't sure that he had any friends. Real friends, I mean. He had lots of kids that hung around him. Mostly kids younger than him and not overly bright. Kids who were impressed with his car and his far-out clothes, and who thought Randy was the coolest guy in town. I guess I'd have to admit I thought that way too, when I got here. I knew better now. Still, that was one incredible car . . .

Of course, he wouldn't have had the car if it hadn't been for his big-shot oilman father who had more money than brains and who thought nothing was too good for his wonderful kid. However much trouble Randy got into, his old man just kept bailing him out and blaming it all on everybody and everything except Randy. That was just the dead opposite of my dad. It seemed he thought everything that ever happened *was* my fault. One thing for sure, though, Randy's dad never would have believed how Randy, who had never worked a day in his life, paid for all the gas he burned in that car. He must have burned a lot of it too. Since he'd been politely kicked out of school a few months back, it seemed like he spent about eighteen hours a day just cruising. I don't think he minded being kicked out of school much.

He wasn't exactly the studious type, and now he had more time to "do business."

I leaned back, trying to get comfortable in my compressed position, and took a deep breath. Wow! A lot of Randy's business had already gone up in smoke. He must be cutting into his profits quite a bit. Breathing the air in that car was enough to get you a second-hand high. I could almost feel that smoke settling into my damp clothes. I'd probably end up going home smelling like a grass fire in a marijuana field. And wouldn't that go over just great with my dad?

But I'd worry about that later. Right now I was listening to that big motor roar. Even over the sound of the music I could hear the pure power as Randy clutched, shifted, and hit the gas again. I looked out the window at the trees along the road. All I could see was a green blur. This was really cruisin'!

Then Randy interrupted my train of thought. "So, what's happening back in Swaziland High?" he yelled over the tape deck. That question was typical of Randy's mentality. It was way back last year when some turned-off high school kids had spray painted that name across the front doors because, according to them, Alderton was about as far out of it as Swaziland. I don't know where they got the idea, probably from some TV show. I doubt if they thought it up themselves. None of them could have found Swaziland on a map if their life depended on it. Anyway, for about two months after that, everybody called it Swaziland High — until the joke wore off. But Randy still thought it was the height of cool to call it that.

"Same as usual," I answered, not wanting to be bothered carrying on a conversation at the top of my voice.

I guess Randy didn't think I was very interesting because he turned his attention to Lance then. "Hey, I got some real good grass left over this time. You interested, Ducharme?'' He asked the question quieter so the music nearly drowned it out.

Lance shook his head. ''No thanks, Randy. I don't need any of that stuff.'' He said it real cool and laid back but I caught the angry flash of his eyes. I already knew he wasn't too impressed with Randy's pot paradise but, even if I hadn't known, that look would have told me.

Randy shrugged. ''Okay, whatever you say,'' he said, but I could tell he was kind of mad about it. He didn't make me any offers and that didn't surprise me. You come under a whole special set of rules when you're a cop's kid. Randy might not be too worried about trading a little dope in front of me but he wasn't about to send me home with the evidence.

He wouldn't have needed to worry. I wasn't about to touch the stuff. I had my reasons—and they didn't have anything to do with my dad being a cop.

Then, the big Silverwind Ranch sign loomed up on the right and Randy hit the brakes. We skidded to a stop and Lance climbed out. ''Thanks for the ride, Randy,'' he said.

''I'll get out here, too,'' I said quickly. I didn't think Dad would be home from work yet but I wasn't about to take the chance of having Randy deliver me right to my doorstep — and right into my dad's waiting arms.

''Okay,'' Randy answered. Then he added, ''The offer still stands, Ducharme. Anytime you think you can handle the stuff, let me know. I can get some really mean stuff for just . . .''

Lance shut the door.

The heaviest part of the shower had already gone over but there was still a lot of water on the road. As Randy pulled back onto the highway and took off, the Corvette almost disappeared in the spray those wide tires threw up. Lance leaned on the gatepost and watched the fading white dot sizzle down the pavement and out of sight. He shook his head. "Next time, I think I'll just go ahead and get wet. Pneumonia won't kill you any faster than Randy's driving."

I gave him an unbelieving look. "Hey, Geronimo. It's me you're talking to. The guy whose fingernails are eaten to the bone from riding in that four-wheel drive with you when you're trying to set the world's landspeed record hauling cow salt across the pasture. Don't try to tell me that fast driving makes you nervous."

"It doesn't — when *I'm* driving. Then I'm in control. I know I can slow down anytime I want to. But I can't control Randy and I'm not sure he's even in control of himself. And things that I can't control are what scare me."

4

I knew I should be getting home but I didn't want to go. I stood there in the lane, looking around and, for about the thousandth time, envying Lance because he lived here. Silverwinds always had that effect on me. To me, this place was what the word "ranch" was all about. It was big — by far the biggest ranch around — about a thousand acres owned outright, and twice that in grazing lease out west in The Valley.

But there was a lot more to Silverwinds than just land. The whole ranch layout, the buildings, corrals, everything — it was all pretty impressive. As well as the twenty-stall horsebarn, a lot of cattle sheds, hay shelters and miles of white-painted fence, there was an indoor horse-training arena — something you sure don't see on the average ranch. But then the average ranch doesn't need an arena. Silverwinds did. When a big part of a ranch's business is raising rodeo stock, it helps to have a place to try those bucking horses out. Between that and just plain training saddle horses the arena got used a lot.

The houses were way back at the end of the lane, protected from the wind by a big hill that rose up behind them and a grove of big pine trees in front. The first time I had seen that main house I could hardly believe it was real — I mean real in the sense that somebody actually lived in it. What it looked like was the kind of house that those rich, mean families on shows like Dynasty live in — huge, classy and expensive. It was lived in, though. At least some of the time it was lived in, when Frank Gillette was home.

Lance and his dad lived in the old house — the log one. It had been built about forty years ago by Silverwinds's former owner, and although it was nothing like Frank's house it was still pretty nice. And it was a real ranch house. While the Gillette place looked like transplanted southern California, the log house looked right for its surroundings. Like it belonged there with its weathered silver-brown sides blending into the land around it.

Frank Gillette owned Silverwinds; Mike Ducharme just managed it for him. I don't know why I put that "just" in there. There was no "just" about the job he did on that ranch. Three good men couldn't have replaced him and if he had ever decided to leave I'd bet the place would start falling apart inside of a week. Frank, on the other hand, could and regularly did take off for a couple of months at a time without it rocking the boat any.

Sometimes I thought that Frank didn't realize what he had in Mike, but then again maybe he understood Mike all too well and played that knowledge for all it was worth. Because, for all Mike's ability with handling animals, he couldn't handle people at all. He was one of the shyest men I had ever seen. At home, or with just a few people he knew really well, he was fine. He could tell some great stories and his sense of humour was almost as crazy as Lance's. But get Mike among strangers, especially people who he thought were a lot smarter than him, and he just froze up. Actually, I thought Mike Ducharme was a lot smarter than most of the people I knew but he wasn't "educated" smart. Lance told me Mike had quit school way back in junior high for some reason and now he thought of himself as ignorant. He stayed as far away from school as he could now — never even went to parent-teacher interviews. He'd been able to get away with it so far because Lance's marks had always been okay and, in spite of the fact that Lance could get into more mischief than a bear at a barbecue, he'd never got into any real trouble at school.

Frank Gillette was Mike's exact opposite. In his custom-made Western suits and four-hundred-dollar boots he really did look the part of a big-time rancher and rodeo-stock contractor.

But looking good was what Frank did best. As far as I could see that was about all he did most of the time: look good and talk a good show. When it came right down to actually getting his hands dirty, Frank wasn't usually around. But he could smile and slap people on the back and convince them of what a great deal they were getting while he was actually dealing them out of the shirt on their back . . . .

A guy like Mike was no match for Frank's kind of "smart." Mike just kept on working like a dog and thinking he was lucky to have the job.

I dragged my mind back to the business of going home and had my mouth open to say goodbye to Lance when the barn door opened and Mike came out, leading a big, sorrel mare. He swung into the saddle and she gave a couple of half-hearted bucks before Mike pulled her head up and spoke to her in a low voice. The mare settled into a skittish, stepping-on-eggs trot.

Mike rode her down the lane to meet us. He looked good on that horse. He was a big enough man to need a big horse like that. "Nice horse," I said, admiring the way she moved.

Mike grinned and nodded. "Yeah, I'm kind of sorry she's nearly broke so I'll have to let her owner have her back pretty soon."

"Where you goin', Dad?" Lance asked, setting his books on a fence post and reaching out to squash a horsefly that had settled on the mare's neck.

"Oh, one of the yearlings in the west pasture has a wire cut. I'm going to put some salve on it before the flies get at it. I'll be about an hour, I guess. Can you work out the buckskin and the bay for me? Just ride them a mile or two and then do a few figure-eights in the arena. Watch the bay. He hasn't been taking the left lead the way he should."

"Sure. What's for supper?"

"There's a pot of stew on the stove. You want anything else, go ahead and make it."

Lance made a face. "Sorry I asked," he said. There were probably only two things connected with food that Lance didn't like. One was Mike's stew and the other was doing his own cooking.

Mike started to turn the horse away. He's not even going to ask, I thought. But then he reined in. "By the way, did school run late today?" he asked innocently. But even from where I was standing, I could see the laughter in his eyes.

Lance looked a little sheepish. "For us it did. Miss Cassidy gave us a detention." Mike just kept quiet and waited.

"For skipping, yesterday afternoon." Mike still didn't say anything.

"We went fishing."

More silence.

"So we had to stay in and scrub the washroom walls."

Mike chuckled. "Serves you right," he said. He touched the mare with his spurs and she moved off at a smooth lope. And that was it. Lance would never hear another word about that incident.

Maybe that sounds like Lance's father let him get

away with murder. But it wasn't like that. Not by a long shot. It was just that Mike Ducharme had his own code of what was important in life. He gave Lance lots of running room as long as he was ready to accept the consequences of the things he did, and the only thing Mike found funnier than us skipping out of Career Fair was the fact that we'd got caught and kept in on a Friday afternoon.

But when it came to something that was destructive or cruel, or downright dangerously stupid, he drew the line and he drew it hard. Lance didn't know much about his dad's childhood but, from the little Mike had ever said, it must have been pretty rough. Mike had been raised by the theory that when a kid did something wrong, he got the belt, and he was raising Lance the same way. Lance didn't get punished very often, but when he did he knew it. And one time last year, the way things turned out, everybody knew it.

It was just after Lance had started smoking, a fact that wouldn't have particularly impressed Mike, but wouldn't have upset him that much either. But for some crazy reason that even he himself didn't understand, Lance lit one up while he was feeding the horses one night. Well, Mike walked into the barn to find him standing there in straw half-way to his knees, with a lighted cigarette in his hand. It was stupid beyond belief. I don't know what made Lance do it — except maybe the fact that despite all the responsibility he'd grown up with, he was still just a thirteen-year-old kid and just as able to make mistakes as any other kid.

If it had been my dad who caught me doing it he probably would have lectured me for half an hour, grounded me for a month, and kept bringing up the subject until I'd have been wishing I'd burned the barn down with me in it.

But Mike didn't operate that way. He twisted right

off then and there and lit into Lance with the first thing he could lay his hands on — which happened to be the end of a lariat rope.

I saw the results when Lance changed for gym the next day. He made good and sure nobody else saw but, by then, we were good enough friends.

What I saw wasn't very pretty. There had been a lot of stuff in the news around that time about social services taking kids from parents who got too physical in their discipline and I figured that one look at Lance would have shaken the fillings out of those social workers' teeth.

"Geez, that must've hurt," I said, feeling kind of sick just thinking about it.

Lance nodded. "Yeah, it hurt, all right. Still does," he added, wincing as he pulled on his gym shirt.

"You don't have to take that," I said, starting to get mad. "This is the twentieth century. He can't —"

Lance cut me off. "Red, there were twelve horses in that barn. You think it would have hurt any less if I'd burned them all to death?"

Before I could come up with an answer to that, Lance was talking again. "Anyhow, Dad didn't mean to get so carried away. He felt real bad about it after he cooled down some."

I guess I still didn't look too convinced because Lance suddenly flashed that grin of his. "Hey, come on, don't sweat it, Red. I had it comin'. It's over. Let's go play some badminton. I might even be stiff enough for you to beat me for a change."

I couldn't believe it. As far as Lance was concerned, the case was closed. What was over was over. It was that simple between him and his dad. No grudges held. Sometimes I wondered if getting things that straight with my dad wouldn't have been worth the odd beating, too.

But it didn't turn out to be case closed after all. Sometime during that Phys. Ed. period, Lance reached for a high shot and his shirt pulled up just as the teacher happened to walk past behind him.

Well, things got pretty complicated before it was all over. The teacher got all excited — and I can't say I blamed him. Even teachers don't exactly go for child abuse. Then the guidance counsellor (the one before Cassidy) and the principal got into the act and it seemed like they were about ready to call in Social Services. Lance felt terrible about the whole thing and kept trying to tell them all to forget it — but it didn't seem like anyone was interested in his opinion. The principal phoned Mike but he just clammed up, refused to come in, or even to talk about it, so that didn't help matters much.

Then, for some reason, Mr. Schafer decided to talk to my dad about it. They'd got to know each other real well during my famous first year in Alderton School and I guess the principal thought that, as an ex-big-city-cop, Dad might have some idea of how to handle the situation.

It turned out to be the right move because, for once, Dad really did know how to handle something. For one thing, Dad had nothing but respect for Mike Ducharme. Not that he thought Mike had been right this time. But he did think Mike was doing a great job of raising Lance and that one incident, as he said to Mom and me, shouldn't be enough to wipe out fourteen years of being a good father.

So Dad went out to the ranch and talked to Mike on his own turf, got his side of the story, took the time to listen to Lance's story, and went back and told Mr. Schafer he was sure nothing like this was going to happen again. The bottom line of the whole thing was that Mr. Schafer took Dad's advice and dropped the whole issue — but not before it had become a pretty good scandal all over the school. On the surface, things between Lance and his dad were the same as ever. He didn't seem to hold it against Mike at all. But I always wondered if, deep down, a little of the trust between them had been broken.

"So, you want to come over tonight?" Lance's voice startled me.

Yeah, I wanted to come over tonight. There was nothing I would have liked better. But tonight was Friday night. I shook my head. "No, I can't make it tonight. I've gotta go to the city with Mom and Dad — to visit some relatives." Why didn't I just come out and tell him the truth? It wasn't that I didn't want him to know. I guess it was just that after all this time of not telling it seemed too hard just to come out with it.

Anyway, that answer was sensible enough to satisfy Lance. "Okay," he said. "See you tomorrow."

"Yeah." I turned and started down the lane. If I hurried I might still make it home before Dad and that would definitely be helpful to my mental health.

5

Mom was already home from work (she's a dental assistant) when I finally got there.

"Hi," she said casually. "Miss the bus?"

"Well, sort of," I stalled, deciding how much I should tell. Mom isn't usually too unreasonable so I figured the truth wouldn't be a bad idea. "Actually, I had a detention."

Mom stopped tearing up lettuce and raised her eyebrows. "Oh," she said with interest. "Care to tell me why?"

Did I have a choice? "Oh, we skipped out of Career Fair yesterday afternoon and went fishing," I said, trying to make it sound unimportant, which, in my opinion, it was. And then, just so she'd know I'd already been sufficiently punished, I added, "So we had to stay after school and wash the bathroom walls."

She looked pleased over that. "And 'we' is you and Lance, I presume?"

I nodded and then asked the inevitable question. "So, are you going to tell Dad?"

She sighed and went back to tearing lettuce for awhile before she answered. "No, I suppose not — not this time."

"Thanks —" I started, but she cut me off.

"But don't go getting the idea that I approve of this sort of thing — or that I'm covering up for you against your dad. I just don't think my nerves are up to one of those scenes between you and him tonight."

She poured herself a cup of coffee and sat down at the table, rubbing her forehead as if it ached. When she picked up her coffee, I noticed that her hand wasn't quite steady. She must have had a rough day. (How could it be anything but rough, spending your life looking into people's cavity-stricken mouths? I'd shoot myself first.) Then she said something that made me realize that it wasn't work that was bugging her. It was me.

"Red," she said, in a voice that was more tired than angry, "Why do you have to keep going out of your way to do things that you know are going to upset him?"

I poured myself a glass of milk so I didn't have to look at her when I answered. "I'm not going out of my way. Dad's upset whatever I do, so what does it matter?" I wasn't trying to pick a fight with Mom. I was just telling the truth.

She sighed and took a swallow of coffee. "I don't know what to do any more," she said. "Sometimes just living with you two is like being caught in the middle of a battlefield. And," she added, her voice tight, "I'd like to know when the war's going to end."

"Ask Dad," I said. "He's doin' all the shootin'. I'm just dodgin' bullets." For a second I thought she was going to start to cry, and I felt rotten. It wasn't fair. Whenever Dad really got me down, Mom was the one that heard all the stuff I wanted to be able to say to him.

Neither of us said anything for a minute. Then Mom got up and came over to where I was leaning on the counter, drinking my milk. She put her arm around me. "Oh, Red, I know it's been rough," she said gently. "It's been rough on all of us." She was staring out the window. I knew what she was thinking about too. That hot July night when our neat little family had become unglued.

"Sometimes it must seem like you can't do anything right, Red. But you've got to try to understand how your father feels." I jerked away from her. How many times had I heard that line in the past three years? Too many. Way too many. I was tired of understanding how he felt. I'd been understanding how he felt for a long time now. When was it going to be his turn to understand how I felt? When was he going to stop trying to make me into some kind of an instant replay of Greg? The new, improved model. Not quite so flashy but safer and more reliable . . .

Well, he could forget it. I wasn't Greg. I never had been Greg. I never would be Greg. I could never be that good — or that bad. Greg was my brother, my big brother. He had a five-year start on me by the time I was born and it seemed like I'd been running all my life trying to catch up to him. Until three years ago.

I was like Greg in a lot of ways, sure. But I was like him in the way that the image you see when you look at yourself in a pool of water is like you. I was Greg's reflection — a pale, wavy-edged copy that was nothing on its own. Greg and I looked alike. Enough alike that everyone could tell right away that we were brothers. Greg had red hair too. Not red like mine, though, that you can see a mile away. His was a kind of auburn that shone like a summer-slick horse's hide, dark brown with chestnut streaks that caught the light. And he had blue eyes — deep, clear blue. The kind of eyes that girls sit moaning over in those teen magazine pin-ups. My eyes are grey. Mom says they're pretty, but what can you expect from your mother? Anyhow, they're not movie star eyes.

But it wasn't just looks that my brother had. He had everything. Brains, athletic ability, charm — he never really had to try at anything. It all fell in his lap. Maybe it was too easy. Maybe that was why, by seventeen, he was living a little too close to the edge, playing with fire just to see how close he could come to getting burned. Looking for the big challenge . . .

Well, he found it. He started doing drugs. And I guess when your dad's a top Inspector on the detective squad in Calgary, messing around with that stuff practically under his nose is a challenge. And the crazy part was that Dad never once suspected. Other people's kids — it seemed like he could pick out the druggies a mile away. But not Greg. Not his can-do-anything son. Of course, Greg didn't exactly haul the stuff out at the dinner table. He was smart enough to be careful. But not that careful. I knew about it. He never really tried to keep it secret from me. I guess he figured that his hero-worshipping kid brother wasn't about to turn him in. And he was right, of course. All along, I knew and I never said a word. I still wake up at night sometimes, thinking about that. Thinking about what would have happened if I hadn't been a loyal kid brother. If I had told Mom and Dad. One thing for sure, Greg would have been in a whole lot of trouble. But, compared to what actually happened, it would have been nothing.

Nobody knows for sure what *really* happened, even three years later. "A lack of oxygen to the brain," was what the doctors came up with, but there was a lot more to it than that. Angel dust, that's what Greg's best friend Rod Caley said they'd been on that night. PCP. I've read a lot about it since, and it's scary stuff. Unpredictable. Especially since most of the time it's not pure. Cut with any kind of other garbage to make it go farther.

Anyway, whatever went wrong, Greg just quit breathing. His friends got him to the hospital pretty fast — considering how high they all were. But it wasn't fast enough — and it was too fast. The doctors saved his life. But they didn't save him.

I'll never forget the first time I went with Mom and Dad to the hospital to see him. I don't know what I was expecting — that he'd look different, I guess. Scarred or tore up somehow. But I was wrong. He looked fine . . .

One time when I was digging fishing worms in the backyard of our place in Calgary, I found a smooth, shiny brown caterpillar buried in the loose soil. That is, I thought it was a caterpillar. But, when I picked it up, it was hollow. Just a preserved skin, shed and left behind. Every segment in place. Every detail perfect. But, empty.

Greg was like that. The face was the same. The body was still there. It breathed and moved. But Greg wasn't there. And it was obvious he wasn't coming back. Not ever.

I couldn't believe how much Mom cried. She cried when she first saw him. And for months afterwards I'd walk in on her unexpectedly and find her sitting alone, crying.

Well, I did some private crying of my own. I was so mixed up. My feelings for Greg were something I couldn't sort out. I knew I loved him but I wasn't so sure I hadn't hated him a little too. Maybe a lot of people feel that way about their big brothers, but I sometimes used to wish that something would happen to him. Something to slow him down a little and give me a chance. But not this.

Mom and I were in bad shape, but we took it well compared to how it all hit my dad. He was like a rock that someone hit with a sledgehammer. One minute, hard, strong, unbendable. The next, completely shattered. At first, he totally refused to believe that Greg could have been into drugs. He thought of excuses he wouldn't have swallowed from someone else in a million years. Some strange virus. An allergic reaction to something. Anything but the truth. Then there was the inquiry, and it all came out. The results of the blood tests showed there was a whole lot more than vitamins in Greg's bloodstream. And half a dozen people, myself included, swore that Greg had been a walking drugstore.

I guess Dad believed, then. But he never accepted. He still hasn't. He still thinks that one of these days, on one of these traditional Friday night visits that we have to make, no matter what, we're going to walk into Greg's room and he's suddenly going to focus those beautiful, empty blue eyes and say, "Hi, everybody, what's for supper? Oh, and by the way, what did I miss the last few years?"

Well, Dad can think that if he wants, but I don't buy it. The doctors don't even believe it. Irreversible. That's the word they use. Irreversible brain damage. They've told that to Dad but he won't listen. He won't listen to anybody.

The crunch of gravel in the driveway brought me back out of the past. A car door slammed and there was Dad, in person, striding up to the back door. The door opened and he came inside, seeming to fill the room — partly because he's a big guy but even more because he somehow commands respect, radiates power like he's surrounded by a force-field or something. People always look up when Dad comes into a room.

"Hi, Ken," Mom said, going to meet him. "Dinner will be on in a few minutes." That was Mom for you. Always looking after everyone but herself. As she walked across the room, the late afternoon sun caught her red-gold hair making it shine like copper. She was one good-looking lady I thought. I wondered if Dad appreciated her. Maybe he did. At least he wasn't always nagging at her like he was at me.

He bent to kiss her. "Don't rush, Kate. You look tired. Hard day?"

She sighed and smiled. "No, not that bad. Just the end of a long week," she said.

It's Friday, Dad, I thought angrily. Of course it's a hard day for her. You should know that. You're the one that makes it hard. You and your pilgrimages to see Greg.

Maybe my thoughts showed on my face. I was probably shooting daggers out of my eyes. Anyway he turned to look at me and, sure enough, he launched right into it. Lecture Number 212. "Red, I thought we had an understanding that you were to start the dinner when you got home from school. You've been home nearly two hours and your mother still has to come in and begin from scratch. What's the big idea? What have you been doing all this time? Watching TV again?"

"No," I said, meeting his glare with one of my own. "I haven't been watching TV." There had been times I had missed starting dinner for no better reason than that. But this time it wasn't my fault. I couldn't make dinner if I wasn't home. I had my mouth open to say that but I shut it, fast. The mood Dad was in the last thing he needed to hear was that I'd had a detention.

He shook his head disgustedly. "Well, then I don't know how you manage to waste time. Obviously it isn't on schoolwork, the kind of marks you've been getting. And," he swept his arm in the direction of my two library books that were lying on the counter, "I suppose this is your idea of a heavy weekend's studying."

I hated him so much right then. And it was all so

predictable. Put Dad and me in the same room for two minutes and he was on my case for something. My marks. That was one of his favourite topics. And it wasn't that they were all that bad. That was what really burned me. I mean, my worst was 65, and that was math which makes absolutely no sense to me. I wouldn't know an integer from an intersection. But I tried. I really did. Well, most of the time . . .

I know I'm not the first kid who ever felt like his dad was picking on him but I guess it's harder for me to take because it didn't used to be this way. All through elementary school I got pretty good marks — good, not great — and I never sweated enough to do any better. But Dad never complained. I'm not sure he even knew exactly what I was doing. Oh, we got along great, a whole lot better than we do now. He just accepted me for what I was, an ordinary kid. He liked me.

But he was crazy over Greg. Greg the Great. The kid who could leap tall buildings in a single bound. Dad's whole life was wrapped up in Greg.

Then, overnight, Greg wasn't around anymore. Well, like I said, it just about destroyed Dad. I'm sure it would have destroyed a lot of guys. But Dad wasn't the sort to lie down no matter how hard he got hit. He came up fighting with all he had left — which turned out to be me.

It was unreal. I mean, I spend twelve years as second-string son in the Cantrell house. No pressure. No sweat. No big expectations. Just hang around and be Greg's kid brother. He'll do the spectacular stuff.

Then suddenly, like magic, I'm supposed to take over being Mr. Perfect. If my marks are in the 80s, why not the 90s? If I come in second in a tough race, why didn't I care enough to train harder and win? It was that way with everything. That kind of culture shock is hard to take. But I think I might have learned to live with it. Who knows, after a while I might even have kind of liked being expected to be something special, once I got used to the idea.

It was the other side of it that I couldn't handle at all. The suspicion. You know how, in the cop shows, they always talk about having the suspect "under surveillance"? Waiting for him to make the wrong move so they've got an excuse to pounce on him? Well, I guess I was the suspect because it seemed like Dad had me under surveillance twenty-four hours a day. I knew why he was doing it. He had trusted Greg. Trusted him a long way. And look where it had got him. He wasn't about to make the same mistake with me.

All at once, I couldn't believe what he was doing to me. There I was, a street-smart city kid who'd been pretty well free to come and go as I liked, within reason, for a couple of years. Then he throws a set of rules at me that would have embarrassed a nursery-schooler.

Like the time he picked me up from the arcade in the neighbourhood shopping centre and drove me home, in a cop car, yet, just because I was fifteen minutes late. I think that was when I started to hate him. And the tighter he pulled my chain, the more ways I found to wiggle loose. I started getting into trouble in ways I never would have imagined before — just to prove that he couldn't stop me. It turned into a full-scale war betwen us. Which is how we ended up in Alderton . . . .

My dad, Inspector of Detectives Ken Cantrell, one of the most respected cops on the Calgary force, just up and quit one day. Quit and got himself a new job as town cop in some god-forsaken place I'd never heard of before. Sold our house in Calgary and moved us to an acreage just outside Alderton. *That's* how far my dad was willing to go to keep me away from the trouble he was sure I was going to find in the city if I kept looking long enough. I guess I should have appreciated him caring that much about me. But appreciation was not one of the emotions I was feeling toward my dad right then.

Or right now, for that matter. Now he was glancing out the window, and before he even turned around I knew he'd found a whole new subject to belly-ache about. "Red, you haven't even got the horses and calves fed yet. You know that we always eat early on Fridays so we can get going as soon as possible. Now those chores still have to be done and —"

"Don't worry about it," I burst out. "You can go as soon as you want. I'll do the chores after you're gone."

He looked at me for a minute, letting the meaning of the words sink in. Then he shook his head. "Oh, no," he said. "Don't try it, Red. You are a member of this family and you're coming to visit your brother just like you always have. Don't get any other ideas."

"No, I'm not," I said stubbornly. "I don't know why you call it visiting. He doesn't even know we're there. Do you know how many evenings I've spent sitting there counting the holes in the ceiling tiles in that stupid hospital? A hundred and seven. A hundred and seven visits to my brother, who might as well be dead. Well, you can go for a thousand if you want. But not me. I can't take it any more."

Dad's face went white and he took a step toward me. "Don't you ever —" he began, and I really thought he was going to deck me. My dad, who never hit his kids.

It was Mom who stepped in and stopped him.

"Let it go, Ken," she said quietly. "Let's not destroy what we've got left of this family."

Suddenly Dad looked beaten. He didn't say another word to me that night. He just turned and walked out of the room, leaving me wondering why getting my own way didn't feel as good as it should have. I started to help Mom with dinner.

An hour later, I stood and watched them drive away. For once on a Friday night I was free. And, feeling incredibly guilty. And lonely.

I finished the chores and then I phoned Lance.

"Hi. I decided not to go visit those, uh, relatives with Mom and Dad after all. What are you doin'?"

"Nothin' much," he said, crunching something that sounded like either an apple or a taco chip in my ear. "Want to come over?"

"Yeah."

6

By the time I had walked down to Lance's place it was starting to rain again. But that was all right. We weren't planning on going anywhere and there was something special about that big, old log house on a rainy night. It always gave me the feeling that I'd gone back in time and landed right in the middle of a Louis L'Amour book, and that we were somewhere in the Old West. If I'd have walked in and found Lance playing poker with Butch Cassidy and The Sundance Kid it wouldn't have surprised me much.

Butch and Sundance weren't there tonight, though. Neither was Lance's dad. He had taken a load of cattle into Calgary and wouldn't be home until late. Just Lance and Tomte, his big, old three-legged cat, were home. Tomte was sitting on the table, washing his face and looking out the window. That's when I knew for sure that Mike wasn't home. He had a few rules for Tomte and they included getting thrown outside if he got on the table. But Lance spoiled that cat rotten. He could have left paw prints in the butter for all Lance cared. The cat had it figured, too. He usually jumped on the table about two minutes after Mike went out the door.

There was a nice little rainy night fire glowing in

the fireplace and Lance was lying on the floor in front of it, drawing of course. He can draw anything. Really. In the two years I've known him he's gone through a lot of different phases with his drawing. First, it was all the usual stuff that junior high kids are into drawing — you know, hot cars and motorcycles. Then, last year, it was Conan the Barbarian, Bruce Lee, all those macho guys with lumps of muscle all over them — the kind of guys us skinny kids wish we were.

A lot of kids practise until they get real good at drawing some special type of picture, and some can copy another picture just about perfect. But with Lance it went a lot farther than that. He drew mostly from his imagination and these days he was doing mainly just birds and animals. It seemed like he had a special feeling for them that he put into his drawing and when you looked at one of his pictures you could almost tell what the animal was thinking.

This time he was working on an eagle. It was soaring high above a rocky ledge and, far below, you could just see the thin thread of a creek winding across the valley. I knew that place, and I knew that eagle. It was back in The Valley where Lance and I go camping all the time. Every time we come over that ridge that eagle flies down from her nest and screams at us. Telling us to get out of her territory, I guess. I don't really blame her. She's got a better right to that country than people will ever have. I just hope she gets to keep it.

Just looking at that picture, I could hear the sound of that wild, defiant scream. It sent a shiver up my back. That had to be his best drawing yet.

Lance had hollered "Come in" at me without even looking up and he was still so preoccupied with the picture that I had to resort to making conversation with Tomte. He's a pretty good talker, for a cat. What he lacks in vocabulary, he makes up for in tones of voice. Finally, though, he got bored and went to sleep so I picked up a wobbly old Rubik's cube off a shelf and went and flopped down on the couch behind Lance. The TV was on. I don't know why. Lance sure wasn't watching it. If it had been at my place, Dad would have been on my case about it in two seconds flat. I could almost hear him. "If you're not watching it, turn if off. You don't need to waste electricity just to provide background noise."

But at Ducharme's the TV was always on, even when Mike was home. I'm not sure why. Maybe they turned it on for the same reason mountain climbers climb mountains — because it was there. Or maybe it was because there were just the two of them in that big house and they could use the company.

Right now there was some kind of a country music show on. I took a glance at it once in a while but it wasn't my kind of music. I sat there, twirling the cube around, aimlessly, finding out for the thousandth time that I have no sense of spatial relations — or whatever it takes to make all those crazy squares line up right.

Mostly, though, I was just watching Lance draw. Looking at his hands, I'd always heard that old line about artists having such special hands but this was the first time I had ever related the idea to Lance. Lance is pretty big and raw-boned, and about as delicate as a bull moose — except for his hands. And they could belong to a surgeon or a concert pianist. Just watching the way he held a pencil, I could tell he was something special.

The voice of the MC on the TV show broke into my thoughts. "And now, ladies and gentlemen, what you've all been waiting for . . ." I strongly doubted that this was what I'd been waiting for but I glanced at the screen as his voice was drowned out by a roar of applause and a lot of ear-piercing whistles.

A girl with long, dark hair and a skin-tight white satin suit was walking across the stage. Wow! Country music was developing a certain appeal all of a sudden! She picked up the microphone and started belting out some tear-jerking cheating song and I started to really pay attention. Country or not, this chick could sing. Then the camera zeroed in for a close-up of her and I forgot all about her singing. I whistled and nudged Lance with my toe. "Hey, get a look at her!"

"Yeah, yeah," he muttered without looking up, his mind still on the wing-feather he was shading. "I've seen your taste in chicks before. Most of them should be locked up in cages at the SPCA. Now, if she looked like Bo Derek . . ."

"She looks better than Bo Derek. On a scale of one to ten, she's at least an eleven."

Lance added one more pencil stroke and smudged it with his finger to blend it in. The girl finished the song and the MC started talking again. "Isn't she something, ladies and gentlemen? Nashville's latest sensation in person, on tour here in Alberta for three whole weeks! And on June 12, mark that date on your calendar, folks — she'll wrap it all up in concert, right here in the Calgary Saddledome! Let's have a big hand for her — the one and only Anne-Marie Charbonneau!"

Lance did look up then — and froze. He didn't say a word. He didn't move. Just stared at that screen like he was seeing a ghost. I didn't know what was wrong with him. For a second I wondered if he was having a heart attack or something. But I never heard of anyone having a heart attack when they were fifteen.

Whatever it was, it was scaring me. "Hey, come on, Lance, so what do you think of her?"

He never took his eyes off the screen but, slowly, he stood up. The pencil dropped from his hand and bounced away under the couch but Lance never noticed. Then suddenly he turned and glared down at me, his eyes blazing dark fire. "I hate her!" he yelled. "I hate her guts!"

He turned back toward the television, swept one more defiant glance across it, swore, and bolted for the door. He plunged out into the rain and the night, slamming the door behind him so hard it sent Tomte into a terrified dive for cover under the table. The cat crouched there, peering out with a bewildered expression on his whiskery face. I understood exactly how he felt. I couldn't believe what I had just seen, either. That had been Lance? Good-natured, easy-going Lance, who'd just as soon donate blood to a mosquito as go to all the trouble of swatting it?

Still half-stunned, I got up and followed him outside. The rain had nearly quit and the clouds were starting to break up. Lance was standing by the barn, leaning over the fence and staring into the darkness. "Hey, Geronimo," I said, coming up beside him, "what was that all about?" He didn't answer. I wasn't even sure that he'd heard me. "What's the matter with you, anyhow?" I said, not sure if I should be getting mad or worried. He turned toward me then, and I got a good look at his face — as cold and hard as chiselled rock.

"Don't push it, Red," he said in a voice that matched his face. And, for once in my life, I had sense enough to shut up.

We stood there in silence for a few minutes. I kept waiting for him to get ready to explain. But, at last, I realized that he wasn't going to explain, even if I waited all night. I gave up. "I guess I'd better be getting home," I said.

Lance turned to look at me then and, for a second, I thought he was going to start talking to me. But he just said, "Okay," and turned away again. Whatever was bugging him, I could tell he wasn't mad at me. But I still felt hurt. He sure wasn't saying anything, though, so I slowly turned and walked away.

Now that the rain had stopped, it was nice out, cool but not cold. And with that fresh, clean-earth smell that always follows a rain. I walked along the lane, scuffing gravel with the toes of my runners, staring at the ground and trying to figure out what had struck Lance. Suddenly something gleaming dull gold in the wet gravel caught my eye. I bent down and picked it up. Lance's St. Christopher medal. He sure wouldn't want to lose that. I dried it off on my shirt and then looked at the chain. In the bright moonlight, the break showed up real clear. It was snapped, right in the middle. That was strange. It was a heavy, double-linked chain and I'd seen Lance wear it through everything from swimming in the river to wrestling calves at branding time. As far as I knew, he never took it off. It would take quite a pull to break it right in half like that. Weird.

But, come to think of it, it had been that kind of a night. I turned around and looked back at Lance. I almost hollered to him that I'd found the medal — but I didn't. He was still standing there, head down, leaning on the fence, lost in some private world. And right now I was shut out of that world. Tomorrow things might be different.

7

The phone rang while I was eating breakfast. Mom answered it. "Hi," she said, her face lighting up. "How's the Chocolate Cake Kid?"

Lance. I think my mom would have adopted him in two seconds flat if she ever got the chance. After all those years of being programmed for mothering two she had a lot of warm fuzzies left over. And, Lance not having a mother, it worked out pretty good for both of them — especially since Lance would die for chocolate cake, which was her specialty. Me, I don't even like the stuff. I like Angel Food, which Mom says is totally out of character for me.

Mom was still on the phone. Either she was talking to herself or Lance was feeling a lot more sociable than he had last night. Finally, she said, "Yes, he's right here, eating as usual."

"Hi," I said, around a mouthful of toast.

"Hi," Lance said, and then sort of hesitiated. Now he's going to explain about last night, I thought. I was wrong. All he said was, "I forgot to ask if you still wanted to go camping in The Valley tonight. Do you?"

"Sure," I said. I'd already cleared that one with Dad so there was no way I wanted it to go to waste.

Anyway, I think I could spend the rest of my life back in The Valley if I had the chance.

"Okay, I've got to help Dad build some fence but we should be done about three. Come over sooner and help if you want."

Now if my dad had wanted me to help him to build a fence, I would have considered it slightly less fun than breaking rocks on a chain gang. But I didn't mind working for Mike Ducharme. He was about as different from my dad as up is from down. He didn't lecture you all the time about how to do things. If you asked questions, he answered them. If you didn't ask, he let you figure it out for yourself. I guess that was one reason why there wasn't much around that place that Lance didn't know how to do by now. And, since I'd started hanging around over there, I'd learned a lot, too.

"All right. I'll come over right after lunch. It's my turn to bring the grub, isn't it?"

"Yeah, and don't forget to bring the eggs this time."

Eggs! Lance couldn't go camping without eggs for breakfast, of all stupid things. And since my horse was more predictable than his, I always got to carry them. Last time, I'd had them in my saddlebag when Pepper stepped in a wasps' nest. Well, that's one time when no horse is predictable . . . We had eggs, all right. I even had them in my hair by the time that horse finished unwinding.

I opened my mouth to tell him I wasn't bringing any dumb eggs but the words never got said. Suddenly, there was a clank that sounded like somebody had dropped a rock on the phone. "You fall off your chair or something?" I asked.

"That wasn't me," Lance answered. "I thought it was you."

"Here comes the cookie monster," a shrill voice cut in. That definitely was not Lance — I hoped.

"I'm Oscar the Grouch," chimed in a second voice, and then I realized that we had been attacked by the Gremlins — Cindy and Cissy Willmore, our next-door-neighbours' four-year-old twins. Cute little monsters, all blonde hair and innocent blue eyes — on the outside. But believe me, that was only a disguise. At heart they had green skin and fangs. And their favourite sport was "interrupt-the-party-line." It had been enough of a culture shock for me to find out that when you lived in the country you shared a phone line with three other houses, but when one of the houses contained the Willmore twins, it was almost too much to take. I don't know where their mother was while they were doing their regular talk-shows but they seemed to always have lots of chances to talk, and once they got on the line it was next to impossible to get them off. I mean, arguing with a four-year-old who's singing nursery rhymes in your ear . . . .

"See yu', Red," Lance yelled. Then I heard him hang up. I sighed and banged the phone down in what I hoped were the Gremlins' ears. Lance had got in the last word on the eggs again.

"You guys still going camping?" Mom asked.

I nodded and gulped down the rest of my milk.

"The weather forecast is for showers. You might get wet."

"We've been wet before. We don't melt."

She gave me a kind of worried look and started to say something else. But suddenly she stopped herself, came up with a smile and said, "Okay. Take lots of food. I nearly blew the grocery budget stocking up for you two bottomless pits. And this time, *I'll* pack the eggs. When I get done with them, they'll be safe in an earthquake."

"Thanks, Mom," I said. I could have kissed her, but that seemed a bit extreme, so I just gave her a hug on my way to the dishwasher with my plate. Ever since Greg, she's been looking at me with that "What if something happens to you, too?" question in her eyes. I know, if she let herself go, she'd wrap me up tighter than those saddlebag eggs — just as unlikely to get broken and having just about as much fun. But my mom is a pretty smart lady.

I spent the rest of the morning getting ready. That included catching Pepper, which usually takes a while. Pepper is a registered Appaloosa mare who was supposed to have been a motorcycle. I got her for Christmas right after we moved out here — and I hated her. I had wanted a motorbike so bad that year that I used to dream about it. But, of course, that didn't fit into Dad's plans for making me into a wholesome country boy. Wholesome country boys rode horses, the way he saw it. (Actually, I knew more kids around Alderton who own some kind of a motorbike than I ever knew in Calgary. But try telling that to him.)

Anyway, Dad has this thing about motorcycles. Being a cop, he's been there to pick up what was left of too many kids on motorcycles that tangled with cars. He says there's no way it's ever going to be his kid he's picking up. I guess he really is on the level about feeling that way because, come to think of it, that was one thing he never even let Greg have.

Dad spent a lot of money on Pepper. She's a good-looking, flashy Appaloosa, and when he bought her she was old enough to have the sense not to kill a green kid but spirited enough not to let me kill her, either. But I still didn't want a stupid horse. As it turned out, she didn't seem to want me very bad, either. The first time I got on her, I kicked her in the ribs, yanked on the reins — showing off like some hot-shot movie cowboy — and got dumped in a snow-bank. After that, we went back to square one and I discovered that if you want any respect from a horse, you'd better start off by giving the horse some respect, too. Now, after having Pepper for a couple of years, I wouldn't trade her — not even for a big, black Harley 950.

But even if Pepper and I did get along fine now, she still had a few little quirks in her personality (horson-ality?). One was about being caught. You never *ever* let her know you were in a hurry to catch her. Walk right up to her, carrying a halter, and that did it. You kept right on walking. So, you played it cool. You took a piece of baler twine rolled up in your hand, and strolled around the pasture like you were bored to death with horses and were just out picking dai-sies. In two minutes flat, her curiosity would get the best of her, and she'd practically have her nose in your back pocket . . .

It worked again. I had her caught, fed and saddled in half an hour. Then, remembering Mom's weather warnings, I tied my rain slicker on behind my sad-dle, over my sleeping bag. Pepper watched me over her shoulder, showing a lot of white around the edges of her eyes. That always used to scare me. I thought it was a sign that she was planning some kind of full-scale rebellion. But then I found out that it's a breed characteristic and that Appaloosas always show a lot of white in their eyes. Anyway, as soon as I stopped rattling that crinkly plastic around she lost all interest in what I was doing and went back to stuffing herself out of her feedbox.

I was packing the food into my saddlebags when suddenly, the idea hit me. I went into the house and got a jar out of the basement — not a real good jar, because I figured that after I got through with it Mom probably wouldn't want to put jelly in it again. Then, I went outside and got together a little sur-prise for tomorrow.

Right after lunch I said goodbye to Mom, said "yes" in all the right places to all her warnings about being careful, keeping warm, watching out for muskegs . . . I was just glad that Dad had to work today. I couldn't have handled any more advice, especially not from him.

Fortunately, by the time I got to Silverwinds, Mike and Lance were at the stapling-up-the-wire stage of building the fence so I just tied Pepper up and grabbed a hammer. Last time I had helped them fence I'd got the job of pulling the post pounder with the old John Deere tractor they always use for fencing. Well, that job was a piece of cake. Dead easy. Until Mike just casually asked me to back the whole rig up to line it up with a post in the corner. What he didn't casually mention was that when you back a rig like that up, the machine you're pulling usually takes off in the opposite direction from the tractor. Naturally, I ended up with it jack-knifed so bad the tractor and pounder were practically at right angles. That job was a piece of cake all right — layer cake — and I felt like the jelly in the middle!

Anyway, today it only took about half an hour for us to finish stapling up the wire. Then Lance and I headed for the barn to get Spider saddled up.

8

Spider was a blood-bay. A colour so red that it looked hot when the light hit it. Lance always said that Spider should have been my horse since our hair was the same colour. In my opinion, though, that colour looked a lot better on a horse than on a human. And Spider had a black mane and tail and four black stockings that calmed the red down a little.

Anyway, Spider was all Lance's horse. Lance had picked him — well, actually they kind of picked each other — and Lance was welcome to him. There was no way I was about to trade. I don't enjoy getting tossed on my head.

Spider was supposed to be a rodeo horse. Frank Gillette was always wheeling and dealing, looking for new bucking horses for his rodeo string and getting Mike Ducharme to try them out for him. Some of them were unbroken colts but others were saddle horses that had gone sour and taken to bucking for some reason. That's what Spider was, a spoiled saddle horse. He was easy to catch, stood there half-asleep while he was saddled, but when somebody got on him he could unwind like he had a skinful of jumping beans.

The first time Mike tried him out of the chute in

the arena last summer, that horse unloaded him in four jumps—and since Mike had a whole shelf full of saddle bronc trophy buckles, that was fairly impressive. I can still see Mike slowly standing up, spitting out a mouthful of dirt, and then saying admiringly, "That's not a horse. Nothin' with only four legs can go that many directions at once. He's a Spider. A little black and red, eight-legged spider." The name stuck.

But the next time Spider came out of the chute, he came like a racehorse out of a starting gate and did three laps of the arena at a run so smooth that Mike could have carried his morning coffee with him and never spilled a drop.

Mike tried him a few more times but the pattern didn't change. When Spider felt like bucking, nothing would stop him. When he didn't feel like it, nothing would start him.

And, as Mike said, "Fifty per cent just isn't good enough for a rodeo bronc." I didn't understand what he meant at first but the way he explained it made sense. "A horse like that one would be nothing but headaches if Frank put him in his bucking string. Every time he didn't buck it would mean a re-ride for the cowboy. An extra horse and extra time. That's the kind of thing a stock contractor tries to stay away from."

"So, what are you gonna do with Spider?" I asked. "Sell him for a saddle horse again?"

Mike shook his head. "Fifty per cent ain't good enough for a saddle horse either. That horse is pure dangerous. There's only one thing a horse like him is good for . . ." He paused and Lance finished the sentence for him.

"Yeah, a thousand pounds of dog food. Just waitin' to be shipped to the packer," he said angrily and I could understand how he felt. It wasn't fair to kill a beautiful animal like Spider. But there wasn't any choice, no one wanted a horse that was unpredictable. At least that's what I thought at the time.

Then one day a couple of weeks later we were walking around in the corral with Mike looking the horses over and talking about them, when Lance jumped. I looked to see what his problem was and there was Spider, standing behind him, nibbling on his shirt. Not biting, just wanting some attention. For an outlaw, that horse sure was a friendly little beggar.

Lance grinned and turned around to scratch the base of Spider's neck. Spider stuck his upper lip way out like horses always do when you scratch that spot for them. I think that's as close as a horse can come to purring . . .

"How much do you think Frank's gonna get for this one?" he asked thoughtfully.

Mike pushed his hat back and looked the horse over. "For meat? Oh, I don't know. Horses are down a little right now. Two hundred, maybe. It's too bad. He looks like a thousand."

Lance stood there a while longer, just staring at the horse. He had kind of a dreamy, faraway look in his eyes. The last time I'd seen him look that way was when he first saw the new blonde in our class last year. Then he turned to look at Mike.

"Think Frank would sell him to me for that?" he asked as casually as if he were talking about buying a bicycle.

I couldn't believe what I'd just heard. Not about the money so much. The Ducharmes sure weren't rolling in it but I knew that Lance had done a lot of extra work around the ranch — stuff that Frank would have had to hire an extra man for otherwise. And where money was concerned, Frank was no fool. You could get away with paying a kid a lot less than a man. So, Lance had some money.

I wasn't all that surprised that he wanted to buy a horse, either. There were always plenty of ranch-owned horses around there that needed riding — Lance had been helping his dad break colts since he was ten — but it wasn't like having his own horse. I didn't blame him for wanting one. But *this* one?

I could just about picture my dad's reaction if I told him I wanted to buy some schizo horse that no one else in the world would touch. But Mike never turned a hair. He just gave Lance a long, measuring look, sizing him up the way he'd sized the horse up a minute ago. "You could never trust him," he said. "You sure you can handle that much trouble?"

Lance's eyes met his dad's. "With enough riding he'd settle down. It'd be worth a try."

The two of them looked at each other for some long seconds. This is it, I thought. This is where Mike pulls rank and says, "Forget it, kid. I'm not letting you kill yourself with some crazy horse." But I was due for another lesson on the difference between Lance's father and mine. Slowly, Mike smiled. Then, he nodded. "Well, if you were old enough to earn the money, I guess you're old enough to choose your own way of throwin' it away. But you'd better be real careful. You get hurt with that horse and things change, understand?"

Lance nodded. "Yeah, Dad. I understand," he said, and that big, white grin broke out all over his face. "And you're gonna smarten up, ain't yuh, Spider?" He gave the horse a friendly slap on the neck. Spider responded by reaching over and nipping at Mike's new straw Stetson. It sailed off his head and landed in a mud puddle. And that was a pretty good indication of about how Spider was going to smarten up.

On the average he bucked Lance off about two or three times a week. Sometimes it was a bird flying up that set him off, sometimes a shadow across the trail, and sometimes it was nothing at all. He bucked because he felt like it. He was a good sport, though. He always stuck around and waited for Lance to get back on and he never bucked twice in a row. And, as for Lance, he got so used to getting dumped that he'd just get up, check to see that all his moving parts were still moving, and get back on. No sweat.

Except for the time that he landed on a fallen log and cracked some ribs. At least that was his own diagnosis. He sure never went near a doctor. It struck me as kind of funny; Lance, who was generally a lot tougher than I was, was scared to death of doctors and hospitals. Probably because, at least since he was old enough to remember, he'd never had anything to do with either one.

I hadn't been that lucky. I got my appendix out when I was ten and, the last year we were in Calgary, I broke my arm playing hockey — bad enough I had to get a pin put in it. I didn't enjoy the experience but at least now I knew I could handle hospitals. Obviously Lance wasn't so sure.

He didn't tell his dad about it, either. "No way," he said. "You know what he said about gettin' hurt riding Spider . . ."

So for about three weeks Lance pussy-footed around, sore as a centipede with corns, but covering it up good enough that Mike never suspected.

Funny thing, though, at that time of year Mike usually had lots of good hard work for Lance. Stuff like splitting wood and stacking bales. But all the time Lance was healing up I never saw Mike ask him to do anything harder than wash the dishes.

Anyway that was last year. Lance didn't give up on that horse and, finally, after a lot of miles and a lot more fast dismounts, it looked like he was winning. Spider had only bucked once this year, back in the spring when a rabbit shot across the trail in front of him. But that time Lance had managed to stay with him long enough to pull his head up and get him under control. Maybe that was all it took. Maybe Spider wasn't going to play if he couldn't win. Anyhow he hadn't bucked since.

But I still had to carry the eggs.

Mike came in when we were just about ready to go and stood around talking to us and watching us finish getting Lance's stuff packed. Then he disappeared into the house for a minute.

When he came out, he was carrying the 30:30. "This time of year the bears are kinda skinny and crabby out there. Won't hurt to have this along," he said, starting to hand the rifle to Lance. Then, he hesitated, took it back, and jacked the shell out of the chamber. With that slow smile of his, he passed the gun over to Lance. "Wouldn't want you to shoot your leg off if that red devil decides to stage one of his rodeos," he said. "There's still six shells left in the magazine. That's all the shots you're likely to need."

Lance laughed. "Yeah, after that either me or the bear is gonna be long gone, one way or the other." He shoved the rifle into the scabbard on his saddle.

I tried to imagine Lance actually shooting a bear. He was a good shot. I knew that from the couple of times we'd been gopher hunting — although that had been with just a .22 of course. The 30:30 was a different story. As far as I knew, except for target practice, he had only shot that gun once.

I'd been over at Silverwinds the day it happened. Mike was away, delivering a horse to a guy way down south of Calgary and wasn't going to be back until real late. Lance and I were out riding in the horse pasture when we saw one of the yearlings standing off by himself, not moving. We went closer and found out why he wasn't moving. His front leg was broken, snapped below the knee with the end of the bone sticking out . . .

It was one of Frank's horses but he was way off in the States somewhere and since Mike wasn't around, it was up to Lance to make the decision. Not that there was really any decision to make. We went home for the rifle and he shot the colt, quick and clean. I couldn't believe how calm he was about it — until afterward when he looked at that beautiful, dead colt and threw up. "I guess I ain't much good at killin'," was all he said. That was last summer. He hadn't even shot a gopher since.

But maybe, if a big old bear was charging straight at him, he might just suddenly develop some of that killer instinct. In that case, I thought I might develop some, too.

9

It was a hot afternoon and the horses were feeling lazy but we weren't in a hurry so we didn't push them. We just rode along, not talking much, letting the warmth of the sun sink into us. It took an hour or so to get to where the Silverwinds lease started. I got off and opened the gate and we headed the horses up the long slope to the top of the ridge. That was the hardest part of the ride, nearly a mile of narrow, rough trail, all uphill.

We stopped at the top to let the horses get their wind — and to look down over The Valley and all the wild country beyond it to the west. You could see it all from here, right to the mountains. And except for a few scattered bunches of cows and some barbed wire fences, out here it hadn't changed in a hundred years. I think that's what made it so special to me. Sometimes when I was in a real miserable mood, and wanted to make myself more miserable, I'd sit here and look out over all that country, and wonder how long it would be till some progressive developer got hold of it and turned it into something useful — like a shopping centre or an amusement park . . .

But today I wasn't in that kind of a mood. Today I could take life like the animals do, one day at a time.

And with the sun shining, a good horse under me, and my best friend beside me, I felt great. We started down the side of the ridge.

About half-way down Lance stopped. "Listen," he said softly. I reined Pepper in but she didn't like standing lopsided there on the side-hill and all I could hear at first was the jingling of her bit as she tossed her head. Then, I heard what Lance had heard. It was there, all right. Faint and far away, but unmistakeable. The eagle.

I searched the sky, squinting against the hard glare of the afternoon sun. There she was, hardly more than a speck. A moving black speck, soaring on the thermals. Circling and screaming at us. I was glad to see her. Maybe she hated the sight of us, but there was something about her always being there to meet us that made me feel like we were coming home when we came to The Valley.

I turned to look at Lance. He was still watching her. "She looks just like your picture," I said. "Wild and free. Like nothing on earth can touch her."

Slowly, he turned to look at me. He nodded. "Yeah," was all he said.

We set up camp where we always do, on the high bluffs above the creek where we can see the valley below us. It didn't take us long. Our camps are fairly simple. A lean-to made of brush with a tarp over it to sleep under, and a circle of rocks for the fire. We staked the horses out on long picket ropes and let them graze while we cooked supper and ate four hot dogs and half a can of beans each. Then we tied the horses up where we could keep an eye on them, and sat down on the hillside to watch the sun disappear behind the mountains.

Sunset always seems to last longer in The Valley than it does anywhere else. I used to think it was because you get a better view of the sky out here but

I've changed my mind. Now, I think it's because it's so peaceful. There aren't any interruptions. It seems like sunset is the only thing happening in the whole world and the only thing that seems worth doing is just watching it happen.

Slowly, the hot disc of the sun sank out of sight, leaving behind a sky of clear orange. Along the horizon, the scattered thunderclouds turned a dark blue, with orange and silver showing through like fluorescent paint. The sky seemed to stay like that for a long time but, if you watched close enough, you could see that it wasn't really the same at all. Every minute it was changing. I'd tried to describe it once, in a poem we'd had to write for language. I could still remember how it went — probably because I'd got an A on it and almost died of shock.

> Evening comes in softly
> Spreading through the sky,
> Grey moving in
> As the blue begins to die.
> Watch it — watch it closely,
> Always in your sight;
> But who can say the moment
> When Day has turned to Night?

Okay, maybe it wasn't the most brilliant poem in the world. But you know that feeling when all of a sudden the day is completely gone.

It was true again tonight. I couldn't figure out the exact time when night started. But when all the earth had changed to shades of grey, we built up the fire and watched the orange tongues of flame lick hungrily over the dry branches as if they were reaching out toward the last orange glow on the horizon.

There wasn't a breath of wind. No animal or bird noises. Everything was hushed, reverently waiting for the sacred ceremony of day giving the earth to night one more time. I could see why so many primitive peoples were sun-worshippers. Because, when the sun set, the whole world seemed to hold its breath.

I looked over at Lance. He was sitting real still, his eyes on the horizon, his mind just as far away. I wondered what he was thinking. Maybe the same thing I was. We were usually on the same wave length.

I don't think you ever really get to know someone until you spend some time alone with them in a place like this. There were kids back in Calgary that I'd gone to school with for six years. I played hockey with them, went to the movies with them, and just generally hung out with them — but I didn't know them. Because when you're at school or out with a bunch of guys you spend all your time playing a role, being one of the guys, being cool. Fitting whatever pattern you think you're supposed to fit. Too scared to let anybody find out who you really are — inside, I mean. Because the real you might not fit the pattern.

But in a place like The Valley, there aren't any patterns. The horses and eagles and coyotes don't care if you're cool. Out here, you learn to be real. And to trust each other. Lance and I have talked about stuff over a campfire that I could never tell anyone else — and I probably couldn't even tell Lance anywhere but out here. Things like that we both believed in God. Neither of us understood Him, but we still believed He was real. When you've watched a Valley sunset, it's pretty hard not to believe in someone . . .

And we were both scared of dying. Especially of dying in a nuclear war — like almost everyone else is, I guess. That stuff came out one night just at dusk. We had been sitting here by the fire when a big jet roared past above us, and suddenly I found myself telling Lance about the times when I'd wake up in the middle of the night to the sound of a plane above me. And I'd start imagining that it was a Russian plane, full of nuclear warheads — the plane that was going to start World War III. (I know they're years beyond the stage where they'd use anything so ordinary as a plane but, in the middle of the night, you aren't all that logical.)

"I really did that a lot when I was a little kid." I tacked that on a bit lamely, like I'd just admitted to something really stupid and Lance was going to laugh at me.

He didn't laugh, though. He just smiled, almost like he was a bit embarrassed too. "When did you outgrow that?" he asked. "It still happens to me sometimes."

Finding out that I wasn't alone was a good feeling. "I wonder what it would have been like to grow up a thousand years ago," I had gone on, thinking out loud. "Before the human race progressed far enough to blow itself off the earth in one easy step. Do you think kids used to wake up scared in those days?"

Lance thought that over. "Yeah," he said, at last. "They probably did. Scared that some cat like Attila the Hun was going to sweep through their village and burn it to the ground. Or that the plague would wipe them all out. Something. I mean, back then it was ten to one you'd be dead by the time you were 35. I think every civilization has to pay its dues." He paused and I digested all that deep-thinking. Then he added, "But it still doesn't make me feel any better about the sound of planes in the night."

It's funny how, since then, even though there have been some real tense international situations come up, they haven't scared me like they used to.

But there were two things that we had never talked

about — my brother and Lance's mother. I wondered about her a lot. All I knew about her was that she wasn't dead, just gone. And she'd been gone a long time. A couple of times I'd started to ask something about her but Lance gave me a funny look and changed the subject fast. So I never pushed it. If he felt the same way about talking about her as I did about Greg, then no wonder.

Tonight wasn't much of a talking night. I said something a few times and Lance answered but I could tell that was all he was doing, answering. His mind was somewhere else.

The fire burned down to red coals. Somewhere across the river, an owl hooted. One of the horses stamped and lazily rattled a metal snap on its halter. A warm breeze floated in from the west, rustling the poplar leaves above us. Then everything was still.

Just a couple of miles behind us, over the ridge, was a highway with people passing each other to get where they were going faster so they could get bored and wish they were someplace else. A few miles down were stores and people and gas stations and TV sets blasting out commercials. Sitting here, I could hardly believe that all that stuff still existed.

It wasn't just a different place. It was like a different time. An untouched time. With my mind a million miles and a million years away, I picked up a stick and poked at the coals, hardly realizing that I was doing my thinking out loud. "Coming out here is like going way back in time. It's like time never happened. Nothing ever changes."

Lance had been leaning back against his saddle, staring into the fire. I didn't know if he was even listening. But suddenly his voice was hard against the silence. "Things change. And there's nothing you can do to stop them. One minute, life's goin' on, just like it always has, and you think it'll stay that way forever. Something happens, bang, and you know that things are never gonna be the same again. And no matter how hard you try, you can't go back to where you were before. You can never go back."

Suddenly a piece of pine root I'd pushed into the coals caught fire. The pitch in it flared up. The firelight flickered across Lance's face — and I'd never seen anyone look so lonely as he did right then.

I'm sitting right here, I thought. Your best friend, and you still think you're alone. I didn't know if I should be mad or sad. I did know that being shut out wasn't a very good feeling. But I figured that however bad I felt, Lance must be feeling worse. "Hey," I said softly. "What's goin' on, Lance? What's wrong?"

He didn't look at me for a minute. Instead he picked up a dry branch and held the end of it in the fire until it started to smoke. He pulled it out and we watched the tiny red glow against the blackness of the night sky. It looked like a UFO. Then it disappeared into a wisp of smoke.

At last, his eyes met mine. "Last night . . ." he began in a voice so low it almost disappeared into the hugeness of the silence. Then one of the horses snorted.

There's no way on earth to describe that kind of a snort to someone who hasn't heard it. It's no more like an ordinary nose-blowing snort than a scream is like a whisper. This kind of snort is the sound of pure terror. Now the other horse snorted. The same sound followed by the scuffle of hoofs, the uneasy trampling of a nervous horse testing the strength of its halter . . .

I saw Lance's hand reach behind him and come back holding the rifle. Slowly he stood up. I was standing up, too, but I couldn't remember moving.

Both of us knew that there was one thing guaranteed to get that kind of a reaction from a horse.

Bear.

I threw a couple of dry branches on the fire to get

some light. If there was a bear out there, I wasn't planning to trip over him in the dark. The fire flared up, brightening the circle around it but only making the darkness beyond seem blacker.

The snort came again. It made me shiver. "If we don't get to those horses, they're gonna bust loose," Lance said, stepping into the darkness. I followed, wishing there was another gun.

For a few seconds, the blackness was like the inside of a cave. Then, gradually, as my eyes adjusted, I started to see shades of grey with darker shadows. That was worse than the pitch dark. In my imagination every one of those black shadows had "bear" written all over it.

Then we were close enough to see the horses, their shapes standing out a shade darker against the night sky. They both had their heads up, their ears pointed to the west.

Suddenly, somewhere downhill, I heard something crashing through the brush. Moving toward us. Something big. Shivers marched up my neck like columns of army ants on the rampage. Lance raised the rifle to his shoulder.

We were almost within reach of the horses now. I could see Pepper's white spots standing out against her black hide like stars in a dark sky. But that was nothing compared to the way the whites of her eyes showed up. And this time it had nothing to do with her being an Appaloosa. This time it was total panic in her eyes. There was another crash, closer and louder. Suddenly she leaped forward, letting her halter shank go slack. Then she threw up her head and hurled herself backward with all her strength. Twelve hundred pounds of hysterical horse. There was a crack like a shot as the rope snapped and Pepper almost went over backwards, but she collected herself, stuck her head and tail in the air, and started off at a trot. She looked back over her shoulder once, to see if Spider was coming, I guess. When she saw that he wasn't she forgot loyalty and broke into a run.

Spider's rope was pulled taut and he was flinging his head back and forth, trying to break loose. But he wasn't as big as Pepper and his nylon rope was strong . . .

Suddenly, just yards away, a huge, dark form broke free of the thick brush and came lumbering through the scattered trees around our campsite. There was a click as Lance cocked the gun and, out of the corner of my eye, I could see him levelling it at the moving shape. All I hoped was that somewhere he had discovered that killer instinct.

But then he lowered the rifle and I heard him let out a big sigh and then a low laugh. In that same second I understood why.

The bear was a moose. A big old cow, near-sighted and relying on her sense of smell to warn her of danger. With the wind blowing straight from her to us, she had come blundering into camp without even knowing we were there. Now she had seen her mistake and was loping off back down the hill. I was glad. Because there was an overgrown mosquito of a calf trucking along behind her just as fast as his spindly legs could carry him. And, a cow moose with a young calf is not the kind of animal you want to deliberately irritate.

I would have almost as soon crossed a grizzly.

I found myself laughing, too, as my knees went weak with relief. Stupid horses. Terrorized by a moose. I never could figure out why the smell of moose scared them so much but I had seen it happen before. And, of course, with it being dark and them being tied up in a strange place . . .

I turned to say something to Lance — and got the

rifle jammed into my hands. "Hold this!" he yelled, already running for Spider. That was when I realized that we weren't exactly out of the woods yet — but if somebody didn't catch Pepper, fast, she would be out of the woods, and halfway home.

Lance grabbed Spider's halter and spoke to him in a low voice. The horse stopped thrashing around for a second. It was long enough. Steel flashed as Lance slashed the halter rope from the tree trunk with his jack-knife. He grabbed a handful of mane, flung his leg over Spider's back, and, by the time the horse realized he was free, Lance was on, riding bareback and reining him with what was left of the halter rope. "Don't go away!" he yelled at me as they thundered off into the darkness, following the same trail Pepper had taken. God, don't let Spider remember he's a bucking horse right now, I prayed silently.

The hoofbeats faded into the distance and a huge blanket of silence fell over me in smothering folds. Ten minutes ago, the silence had felt good, Now I was cold. I threw a bunch of wood on the fire, making a beacon for Lance to aim for when he came back. (It's funny I didn't also give some waterbomber a beacon to aim for. In the dark I'll bet it looked like the whole forest was on fire.)

I settled down in the warm ring of light, hugging the rifle. Somewhere, a coyote howled. I'd never noticed what a lonely sound that was before.

10

The minutes stretched out and the silence got heavier. A whole parade of "what if's" began to march across my mind. What if Lance didn't come back? What if Spider decided to go to bucking somewhere out there in the dark? What if Lance was lying out there right now with a busted leg or something? And what if a bear really did come strolling up to camp while I was here all by myself?

I checked my watch. 10:43. Maybe math wasn't my best subject but I could figure one thing out in my head. With daylight coming at about five or six this time of year, I had at least six hours of darkness ahead of me. And that sounded like an awful long time.

Then I heard it. The most beautiful sound in the world at that exact moment. The hoofbeats of a trotting horse. Carefully, I laid the rifle down and started walking toward that sound. A couple of minutes later, shapes loomed up in front of me. Two horses. And a rider on the first one. Good old Lance.

He rode up and reined in beside me. "Your horse, sir," he said, in his best English-butler accent, and held out what was left of Pepper's halter rope.

"Thank you, James," I replied, with proper Englisharistocrat dignity, and followed him back toward the fire.

Lance turned back into himself, flashing a grin I could see in the dark, as he said, "Hey, that old mare of yours can run some! She was over the ridge and halfway down the other side when I finally caught up to her. After that Spider got the idea it was a race so we all ran another quarter mile before I could get him stopped with just the halter."

We broke out of the darkness into the firelight and I got a good look at the horses. It had been quite a run, all right. Both of them were shiny with sweat and their manes and tails were tangled with leaves and twigs. Pepper was looking kind of subdued. Her expression reminded me of someone who'd been out at one heck of a party the night before — but this was the next morning.

Lance slid off Spider's sweaty back and gingerly took a couple of steps. "My pants haven't been this wet since I was two years old," he said, disgustedly.

"You meet a bear out there somewhere?" I asked, looking him over. He had a long scratch on his cheek, the back of his shirt was ripped, and a couple more scratches ran across his shoulders.

He shook his head and a shower of spruce needles fell out of his hair. "Nope, a spruce tree. Spider took a short cut and he kinda forgot to leave room for me." He gave the horse's neck a friendly scratch and Spider responded by rubbing his wet, itchy head on Lance so hard it almost knocked him over. "Well, let's get these horses tied up again. I think they've got the kinks out of their tails now."

We found a couple of good-sized poplars a little closer to the fire this time. Spider's halter shank was still long enough to tie and I used the lariat off my saddle to replace Pepper's rope. At last we had everything settled down for the night again.

Lance yawned. "I'm tired," he said. "Let's hit the sack." He threw one last branch on the fire to give us enough light to find our way into our sleeping bags. We crawled into the lean-to and pulled off our boots. Lance spread his horse-sweaty jeans out to dry. "Anything else needs investigating tonight, Red, *you* go," he said, as I climbed into my sleeping bag fully-clothed. The way things had been going so far, I wasn't taking any chances of having to make a fast get-away in my underwear.

Lance took off what was left of his shirt and held it up to the light to admire the big rip across the back. "Looks like it's shirt-shoppin' time again," he said with a grin. Lance was harder on clothes than anyone I'd ever known . . .

Just then I noticed two things. One, he wasn't wearing the medal around his neck — which was hardly surprising since I still had it in my pocket. I was just going to reach for it when the second thing stopped me. There was an angry-looking red mark on the side of his neck. He could have got it just now when he got all the other scratches but, somehow, I didn't think so. It was more like a bruise. Like somebody had taken that heavy chain that held the medal and jerked it so hard it broke.

I lay still, feeling the tension in my muscles gradually seep away into tiredness. The firelight was almost gone but far-off over the mountains the sky lit up as sheet-lightning glowed and then died. I wondered sleepily how much water the lean-to would shed. Everything was so quiet that I could hear Lance's even breathing. He could have been asleep — but I knew he wasn't.

And I couldn't go to sleep until I asked.

"Lance?"

"Yeah?"

"Just before the moose showed up, what was it you were gonna say about last night?"

The even breathing stopped. He half sat up and turned toward me, but he didn't say anything. Then he let out his breath in a long sigh. "Aw, it was nothin'," he said.

I wished I could have seen his eyes then. I can always tell when Lance is lying by his eyes. But, as he lay down again, the light caught his face for a second. It had gone hard again. Marble. Like one of those Greek statues.

I wasn't sleepy any more. I don't know how much longer I lay awake but the last time I checked my watch it was 1:40—and I was wide enough awake to get up and play basketball or something.

"You awake, Lance?" I whispered.

"No," he said. "Shut up and go to sleep."

I woke up to the smell of woodsmoke and the feel of the damp cold creeping into my bones. Reluctantly, I opened my eyes. Grey dawn. And Lance was already up, dressed, had the horses picketed out to graze, and now he was working on a fire. Well, there are morning people and night people . . .

I snuggled farther down into my sleeping bag and closed my eyes. But it was no use. When you're this cold and awake, you stay awake. I wished Lance would hurry up with the fire but he always had to do things the hard way. Now he was down on his knees, blowing gently on a tiny anemic-looking flame that was licking feebly at a little pyramid of spruce twigs. Personally, I thought that a good shot of barbecue starter wouldn't do any harm.

I stuck one hand out, grabbed my jacket, and pulled it into the bag with me to warm it up. When I put my feet into my boots I wished that I could have warmed them up somehow. They felt like they'd grown icicles in their soles.

I shivered my way out of the lean-to and over to the undernourished fire. Lance had added a few sticks about the size of my thumb and now he was busy pouring water into the coffee can. "What time did you get up, anyway?" I asked, yawning.

He shrugged. "A while ago. I woke up and couldn't go back to sleep so I got up." He handed me the coffee can. "Here put this on the fire, will ya?" he said kind of vaguely, like his mind was someplace else.

"Fire? What fire? You call that a fire?" I said sarcastically.

That got his attention. He gave me a sideways look and I knew what was coming. "Paleface build big fire, freeze to death — " he began, doing his movie-Indian routine.

"Indian build little fire, keep warm," I finished for him. If he didn't come up with that line at least once during a camping trip I'd worry about him.

He finished spreading the bacon out in the old, black frying pan and then looked up accusingly. "I couldn't find the eggs. You didn't forget the eggs, did you Paleface?"

"No, Geronimo, I didn't forget the precious eggs. Mom packed them for us herself. They're in a jar in my saddlebag."

"Eggs? In a jar? You mean they're already broke?"

"No, she filled the jar with dry straw and then fitted the eggs in so they couldn't even jiggle. She says it's a hundred per cent guaranteed."

"You know, Red, for such a dumb kid you've got a real smart mother," Lance said over his shoulder as he headed for my saddle which was lying over beside the lean-to.

I gave that comment the amount of attention it deserved — none — and concentrated on getting the coffee can balanced just right so it didn't tip over and drown Lance's roaring campfire.

I wasn't paying any attention to what he was doing

over there until I heard him say, "Hey, how about that, two jars of eggs."

I turned around. He had a jar in each hand and he was peering through the side of one. "This sure don't look like straw," he muttered, holding the jar up to his eye.

"No, not that one —" I started, but I was too late. Suddenly he gave sort of a squawk and let go of both jars. There was a sound of breaking glass and I abandoned the coffee and rushed to the scene of the accident. The first thing I saw was six nice, big, smashed eggs oozing yellowly through the straw and broken glass . . .

The other jar didn't break. Safe and sound inside, happily crawling through the dirt and grass I had packed them in, and leering out the sides of the jar, were the couple of dozen choice dew worms I had dug out of the garden yesterday morning. What a relief! The great Cassidy Fishing Method test was still on. The worms were safe. Who cared about losing a few eggs? Three guesses who cared.

"Worms!" Lance squeaked. "Dirty, slimy, overgrown worms! The eggs are in a jar, he says. So I look in the jar and what looks back at me? A big, gooey, grinning worm! I tell you, Cantrell, this time you've gone too far!"

I didn't answer. I couldn't. I was doubled up on the ground laughing so hard I could hardly breathe. I couldn't stop laughing — not even when the coffee boiled over and neatly extinguished Lance's beloved miniature fire.

We had bacon and water for breakfast. Lance was real grumpy while we ate. Maybe he wasn't a morning person after all.

It was only a couple of hundred yards down to the creek but we took the horses with us and picketed them on the flats where the grass was better and we could keep an eye on them.

We got our fishing rods assembled and I brought out my jar of precious worms. Lance glared at them and muttered something under his breath. I ignored him, selected a choice, juicy one, and baited my hook. Then I passed him the jar. "Care for a dew worm?" I asked politely.

"Never touch the things," he replied, curling his lip. "They give me heartburn." He took the jar and sneered at its occupants. "Anyhow, these aren't dew worms. They're just ordinary earthworms."

"Naw, they're too big for earthworms. Look at the size of those suckers. Anyhow, how would you know they weren't dew worms. You ever seen a dew worm?"

"No. You ever seen a dinosaur?"

"No."

"Well, how do you know that ain't one standin' there with your saddle on it?"

I groaned, and Lance laughed and put a worm on his hook, just like he'd been planning to do all along — after he'd got me thoroughly bugged. Someday I was going to learn not to get caught in those routines of his. Lance's brand of logic could drive anybody crazy — especially teachers. By the time he got done with them they were so far off the topic that someone had to send out a search party.

We spent a couple of hours drowning dew worms — earthworms? Whatever they were, the trout didn't like them. I didn't blame the fish. Those worms were ugly. Anyhow, we didn't even get a nibble.

Then we tried spinners. And when that didn't work any better, we got sick of fishing, found a comfortable spot by the beaver dam and just lay on our stomachs watching the tadpoles and water bugs and stuff. If you keep quiet long enough you can see some real interesting things in the shallow water along the edge. Today's highlight was a fight between a giant water bug and a leech. They really went at it.

They kind of reminded me of the characters that show up on "The Wonderful World of Wrestling" or whatever those Saturday afternoon TV riots are called. The bug won. But he didn't get any trophy or applause. He just ate the loser.

There were some little fish swimming around, too. Not big enough to think about catching. Cute little guys, though. "They must be some kind of minnows, huh?" I asked after awhile, keeping my voice low so as not to scare them away.

Lance answered without taking his eyes off the fish. "Yeah, they're sticklebacks. Funny little critters," he added. "The female lays the eggs and then just takes off. It's the male that hangs around, keeps them all tucked in and safe, fights off their enemies . . ."

Something different in his voice made me turn to look at him and suddenly, as I watched, his face clouded over.

"And their mother's forgot she ever had them. She's out there somewhere, just swimmin' around in the sunshine, looking young and sexy . . ."

Suddenly he reached over and picked up a heavy chunk of beaver-chewed wood that had been lying on the bank beside him. "Stupid fish!" he yelled, and heaved the log into the water. Silver fish streaked in all directions and the water turned murky as the bottom silt roiled up.

Lance stood up. "This is boring. Let's get out of here." He threw one challenging look in my direction, as if he half-expected an argument from me. He didn't get it. In the past two days I'd seen him blow up at a TV show and a bunch of minnows. I didn't plan to be next on his hit list.

We packed up our fishing stuff and headed for the horses.

11

The next few days were fairly uneventful. Dad was still mad at me for refusing to back down about visiting Greg. At least I guess that's what was bugging him. He had hardly spoken to me since that night and I was almost missing having him yell at me. It couldn't have been any worse than the silent treatment.

I stayed out of his way as much as I could which meant I was hanging out over at Silverwinds even more than usual. But things weren't totally great there, either. Lance was still acting weird. Not crazy-weird. He hadn't thrown any more of those tantrums lately. But he still wasn't himself. We'd be working together and I'd turn to say something to him but he'd be staring into space like he didn't even remember I was around. Between him and Dad, I was beginning to wonder if I'd turned invisible or something. And then, one night I found myself wishing I could turn invisible . . .

It was late in the evening. I'd been down at Silverwinds and now I was walking home, just before dark. I heard a car coming and glanced over my shoulder to see who it was. I took a second look. It was that Continental again. In the early dusk, there was something almost eerie about the way that car came cruising along like a silent silver shadow. Why did it keep showing up?

Suddenly a shiver went down my spine. Don't ask me why I had to pick that exact moment to think about a movie I'd seen a few weeks before. *Christine*, it was called. One of those super-gory Stephen King horror shows. This one had been about a car. A real nasty old '58 Plymouth who got her kicks by driving herself around, killing all her enemies very thoroughly and very messily. All at once, I found myself wondering what I might have done to offend an '85 Lincoln.

I could hear the car pulling up beside me now and, honest to God, it was almost more than I could do to keep myself from breaking into a run. My palms were sweating and I could feel my heart pounding. Cautiously I looked over my shoulder. I really think I must have been half-expecting to see a moss-encrusted skeleton behind the wheel. But, of course, it was only the creep. The black-moustached, white-Stetsoned "godfather." Right now, though, he wasn't looking half so creepy. The way my imagination had been running, anybody who was warm and breathing looked just fine.

The guy touched a button and the window hummed open. He stuck out his head (narrowly missing knocking off the hat) and said, "Hold on there a minute, kid. The lady wants to talk to you." His southern-fried drawl sounded like something he had picked up cheap at a garage sale in Georgia.

I stood there gawking while he drove the car onto a side lane to the neighbour's hayfield. He opened the door and got out. I wasn't so sure I liked this deal much. If the woman hadn't been there, I think I would have split — just took off running through the field and never looked back. You hear about some pretty weird stuff going on these days. Even with her standing on the other side of the car I wasn't all that comfortable with the situation. But I was curious.

For all I knew, they could be movie scouts. Maybe at long last Hollywood had realized that all those dark, supposedly handsome guys like Michael Jackson and Matt Dillon were out of it. Maybe red hair was in and I was about to be discovered. Well, maybe not. Anyway, I walked over to the car to see what they wanted.

As I came up, the woman turned to the man and I heard her say softly, "How about taking a walk, Jerry? I'd like to talk to him alone."

The man didn't answer, just sort of scowled, shrugged, and slunk away like a dog who had been sent home. Jerry, whoever he was, had a lot of class — all of it low, in my opinion.

Then I turned to look at the woman and forgot that Jerry had ever existed. She was beautiful — the most beautiful girl I had ever seen. Her hair was black, so black it shone almost blue when the light hit it right, and it fell in loose curls to her shoulders. Her face was thin, almost gaunt, with the kind of high cheekbones models have and girls are always moaning about wanting.

But the eyes are what I'll never forget. They were almost as dark as her hair and when she looked at you it felt like they might melt a hole in you. "See Forever Eyes" — that was an old Prism song I'd heard on the radio last night and it described her better than I ever could. Standing there, leaning on the side of the Lincoln, wearing blue jeans, high boots and a suede jacket, she looked as much a princess as Diana.

At first I thought she was real young — eighteen, maybe twenty. But when I looked closer, I could see that I'd been wrong. Not about her being beautiful;

she'd be beautiful till the day she died. But she wasn't all that young. Something about those eyes said that she'd done a lot of living.

I was sure I had never met her before but something about her was so familiar that it was driving me crazy. Before I had time to think about it any more, she stepped forward. "Hello, Red," she said, like she'd known me all my life.

I just stood there, staring at her.

She laughed. "I've done my homework," she said. "Your name is Jared Cantrell but," she glanced mischievously at my hair, "for obvious reasons, everyone calls you Red."

Well, I couldn't deny any of that and since she already knew the answers, I couldn't think of anything to say. I stood there looking stupid some more.

"And right now, Red, you're thinking, 'Who is this lady and what does she want with me?' Right?"

I didn't have much choice but to answer this time so I sort of shrugged and said, "Yeah, well, uh I guess so." Brilliant. I could have won a public speaking prize for that one. Talking to her, I was so far out of my league I was lucky to remember how to speak English.

She nodded. "Okay, then let's start with who I am."

All of a sudden, something clicked in my memory and, for the first time in what seemed like hours, I thought of something to say. "Anne-Marie Charbonneau," I interrupted.

"How did you know?" she asked, her face a strange mixture of pleasure and concern.

"I saw you on TV. A show called *Country Crossroads* or something like that. Last Friday, I think." Yeah, it was last Friday for sure. That night over at Lance's place, when he —

My train of thought was cut off as she asked, "And

that's all you know about me? What you saw on TV?" She sounded different now. Not so confident. Maybe even a little nervous.

I nodded. "All I know is that you're one of the biggest new stars in Nashville and that you're a real good singer — for country, that is." (I threw that last in to salvage my reputation as a normal, red-blooded, country-music-hating teenager.) She smiled at that but I could tell that something was bothering her.

Something was bothering me, too, but I couldn't seem to put my finger on it.

She gave me a long searching look as if she were trying to decide if she trusted me or not. Then she sighed and looked down at the toe of her boot as she said, very quietly, "Yes, Charbonneau's the name I go by." Slowly she raised her head and those unbelievable eyes met mine. "But it's my maiden name. My legal name's Anne-Marie Ducharme."

My head felt like a computer that was about to blow its circuits. As the name registered I thought, yeah, that's why she looked familiar. No wonder those eyes reminded me of someone. The eyes, and the smile.

Lance Ducharme was the spitting image of his mother.

I don't know how long I stood staring at her before her voice brought me back to reality.

"So now you know."

So now I knew. I knew how Lance could freak out over a name and a face on a TV show. I knew why, overnight, he had changed into somebody I hardly knew any more. And I knew for sure that for Lance, Anne-Marie was bad news by any name she chose.

I couldn't think of anything to say, so it was Anne-Marie who finally broke the silence again. "I want to see my son, Red," she said softly.

Well, I supposed that wasn't so surprising but I

couldn't see why she was telling me — or maybe I didn't want to see why she was telling me. Any way you figured it, I wasn't exactly Lance's guardian. "He lives the next place down on the right," I said, knowing even as I said it that she hadn't gone to this much trouble to get me to give her directions.

She shook her head. "It's not that simple, Red. I can't just walk up to the house and knock on the door. Not after all these years."

I didn't say anything; I stood looking at her, waiting for her to make her next move. But she outwaited me. Finally I broke down and asked, "So, what do you want from me?"

It took her a while to get to the point. "Well," she started slowly, "I've still got some friends around here, and, like I said, I've been doing some homework. Finding out all I can about Lance. And that's why I know all about you. From what I hear, you're about the closest friend he's got."

I nodded. "Yeah, we're friends," I said cautiously, not sure where all this was leading.

She gave me a long, level look. "Then help me. Set it up so I can meet him somewhere and talk to him. Not at the house. Not with his father there. Just Lance and me." She hesitated, giving me some time to take it all in. One half of me smelled danger — that half was still thinking I should have followed my first instinct and taken off. But the other half was weakening, getting caught up in the spell of those eyes. Then she added something that put a whole new light on the subject. "But don't tell Lance that it's me he's meeting," she said.

And instantly the rest of me agreed with the part that was yelling "Danger!" at the top of its voice. According to my code of friendship, you didn't set your friends up for that kind of a surprise party.

"Why don't you want him to know?" I asked, my voice hard and defensive.

"Because," she said slowly, "he might not come if he knows."

"Oh, no," I started, my mind shying away from the whole idea like a horse shies away from a rattlesnake. I could feel my temper starting to rise. "No way are you getting me mixed up in a deal like . . ."

Before I had a chance to finish, she cut me off, her voice suddenly just as hard as mine. "You've got me judged already, haven't you?" she said angrily. "Tried and convicted. You think you've got it all figured out. I left once so I'd better stay gone. That's what you think, isn't it, Red?"

I was stunned. All I'd said, tried to say was more like it, was that I wasn't about to trick Lance into anything. And suddenly she was taking the whole thing like a personal attack. I figured she must be carrying around one giant chip on her shoulder — or a great big load of guilt.

Then before I could think of an answer, she was talking again but she didn't sound angry any more. Her voice was almost gentle as she said, "I don't blame you for thinking that. I just hoped you might be the kind of person who would listen to the whole story before you condemned someone for what they had done in the past." Her voice faded away and she stood silently, just looking at me.

That was enough. I still wanted out of there. I wanted out real bad. But I didn't have a chance. Not with those eyes holding me there.

I met her look. "Okay," I said tiredly, "I'm listening."

12

I leaned against the fender and waited for Anne-Marie to say her piece. It was a while before she got around to saying anything. Maybe she didn't know where to start. What she finally did start with surprised me.

"Do you know what it's like to be poor, Red?" I don't think she expected an answer. She went on before I could think of one, anyway.

"I don't mean can't-afford-a-new-car-poor. I mean dirt-poor. So poor you get your Christmas dress at the Thrift Shop."

It seemed to me this was a long way from the subject she was here to discuss but she kept talking so all I could do was to keep listening.

"I grew up that poor," she said softly. She paused to light a cigarette. I noticed that her hand was shaking a little and I wondered if, inside, she wasn't as cool as she had seemed. "It was way up in northern Saskatchewan," she went on, staring at the smoke that curled from her cigarette. Her voice had taken on a faraway sound, almost as if she wasn't just telling the story any more. In her mind, she was back there, reliving it.

"It's lake country. A beautiful place to visit. But

we lived there all year round. And when you sit out six-month winters when it's forty below for weeks at a time, with five people in a two-room shack, it's pure hell."

She took a drag on her cigarette, pushed back a loose strand of hair, and went on. "My mother was Cree. Sixteen years old and right off the reservation when my father came up from the south, working on a government road crew. He was a drifter. Part white, part Indian, and," she laughed, a soft, bitter laugh, "all useless. But my mother couldn't see that. She couldn't see past his looks. He was handsome. And charming. And he'd been places, seen things . . .

Well, she married him. And, since he wasn't a Treaty Indian, she lost her right to live on the reservation. They moved into a shack on the edge of town. At least, my mother did. My father was away most of the time. Down south working, he said, but we didn't see much of the money he supposedly made. After a few years, he went away for good. He was gone, just like he'd never been there — except that he left my mother four kids to raise. Four kids and her pride. That was all she had. And pride doesn't buy many groceries. She managed to get a job waiting tables at the café in town. I was the oldest so I was left to look after my little brothers."

Anne-Marie stubbed out the cigarette and turned those high-voltage eyes on me.

"I was eight years old, then," she said, real low.

I couldn't believe it. "Eight?" I repeated. "That's not old enough to look after a bunch of younger kids."

She smiled. "I got old in a hurry," she said. "Oh, my mother saw that I went to school. She worked the late shift so I had time to get home before she left. Just time. The other kids would stop to play or, when we got older, buy a Coke downtown. But not me. Straight home to that shack and three dirty, whining kids. It was like being in prison — but the only crime I'd committed was being born in that god-forsaken place." Her voice was hard and it struck me that, more than twenty years later, the anger was still burning inside her.

Then her voice warmed up a little, as if she was dreaming about something that didn't hurt so much. "I used to get the little kids to sleep and then I'd sit listening to the radio. Sometimes I think that radio was the only thing that kept me from going crazy. There wasn't any television up there in those days so the radio was the only proof that somewhere out there was a real world—a world that wasn't all moose meat, mosquitoes, and mud.

"The only station that came in real good was a country one and I listened to it until midnight every night. I knew every song they played and every singer who sang those songs. I used to sing along just to keep myself company. And whenever I got fifty cents I'd buy one of those magazines, *Country Hit Parade* or something they were called, and they were full of song lyrics and pictures of these beautiful ladies with long hair and sparkly gowns. I'd lie there and stare up at the bare beams and I'd swear to God that some-how, someday, I was going to live like that."

She paused and took a deep breath. "I was in junior high when the talent show came up at school. A whole twenty dollars, first prize." She laughed. "Not much to get excited over, eh?" I shook my head but before I could say anything she went on, "But as far as I was concerned it could have been a million. I wanted it so bad. But what I wanted more was just to win. To be somebody. For once in my life to be somebody special. And yet I was so scared to try in case I didn't make it.

"But I did try. I got up there in my best Thrift Shop

dress and I looked right through all those snotty little girls who were looking down their noses at poor little Anne-Marie. I sang 'Your Cheatin' Heart.' I sang it like my life depended on it. And I won the twenty dollars. But that wasn't the best part of it. One of the judges was a guy who had his own dance band. He came up after the show and offered me a job, singing with them. I couldn't believe it. It was like I had been drowning and someone had thrown me a rope.

"My mother said I was too young and asked what the job paid, all in the same breath. The money won. I was fourteen and a singer. I thought the end of the rainbow was coming to meet me."

She laughed. "And then I found it wasn't going to be all rainbows after all. The dances that band played for were more like street fights set to music. By the time I turned fifteen, there wasn't much I hadn't seen — of the rough side of life, I mean. I still hadn't seen anything of what I had dreamed was out there."

"Didn't your mother care about the kind of places you were singing in?" I asked. I mean, *I* was fifteen and I could just see my parents' reaction to me spending my nights in a joint like she was describing.

It took Anne-Marie a while to answer. Finally she said, "I don't know, Red. I never really thought about it. I guess she cared. But with five mouths to feed on a waitress's pay, it would have taken a whole lot of caring for her to make me give up a paying job." She paused and then added, "*If* she could have made me. Because, bad as it was at those dances, they were still the only thing that made my life worth living. They were my one chance to be young. And deep down I think I always knew it was my singing that was going to get me out of that town.

"Then the rodeo came to town. Three days of rodeo and a dance every night. That's where I met Mike Ducharme. He was riding high then. Champion saddle bronc rider. Every girl in the hall was out to get noticed by him but he was real quiet and shy. Mostly he just sat alone at a table by the stage.

"Well, during an intermission, I went over and started talking to him. He was real nice to me. Didn't make a pass at me in the first five minutes like a lot of guys would have done. He came back the second night and we talked some more. I found out that he was part Cree, too, from someplace in northern Alberta.

"The third night, Mike stopped in to say goodbye. He had to get on the road for the next rodeo. We sat down for a few minutes and, maybe it was the thought that the one person who'd ever treated me with that kind of respect was going out of my life, but suddenly I was crying. Crying and telling Mike how I hated that town. How I had to get out of there before I went crazy. He held me until I stopped crying and then he said, 'Do you want to come with me?' That was all. No 'I love you's.' No promises. Nothing but a chance to go. And I grabbed it. Oh, how I grabbed it. I told myself I was in love with Mike. But what do you know about love at fifteen?"

I tried to apply the question, but all I could decide was that I hadn't been in love since Suzie Melton. One thing I did know for sure. There was no way I could choose someone to spend the rest of my life with right now.

Anne-Marie obviously hadn't been ready for that kind of choice either. "I was in love with a ticket out of town," she said with a bitter little laugh. "And," she added, her eyes level and honest, "I used Mike to get that ticket."

"We went by my house and got my stuff. It filled two grocery bags. I didn't have a suitcase. Mom was at work and my brothers didn't seem surprised that I was leaving. I guess, really, I'd been leaving that place since the day I was born. I didn't look back when we drove away. And I haven't been back since."

She stopped and looked like she expected I was going to say something, tell her that she'd done right — or wrong. But how was I supposed to know what she should have done? Me, the original messed-up kid. It's a good day when I can figure out what *I* should do about something . . .

I tried to think what it would be like to leave home at fifteen. To just drive away with some stranger you've known for three days and never look back. Not to know where you were going. Not to have anyone keeping track of you. Anne-Marie had been one tough little girl. I couldn't help but admire that kind of determination to get what she wanted. I couldn't help being a little afraid of it too.

She started talking again and her next words echoed the thought that had just crossed my mind. "I was lucky. Mike was good to me. Better than I deserved, I guess." She *was* lucky the guy she'd picked had been Mike Ducharme. With some other drifter the story might have come to a sudden end — with her dead in a ditch somewhere.

But the story didn't end there. "He kept on rodeoing, following the circuit and winning enough for us to live decent. It wasn't a bad life. I didn't love him and I never really thought he loved me, but we got along. And at least we were free, on the move, seeing the country. But," she sighed, "nothing ever stays the same. By the time I was seventeen we were married and I had Lance. Mike had got busted up pretty bad a couple of times riding broncs and the money was scarce. Then Frank Gillette hired him to help handle his rodeo stock at a couple of rodeos and by the time we came to Alderton, Frank had decided he wanted Mike to work for him full-time at Silverwinds.

"Mike took the job and we settled down. I should

have appreciated it. I'm sure he did it mostly for me
—and Lance. So we'd have a home and some security
— Mike could have lived on nothing the rest of his
life and never care much.

"But I didn't appreciate it. I hated it. The world was
closing in on me again. I was back in a nothing town
with a nothing future. Back where I'd started. And
with another baby to look after — this time my own.
The world I'd left home to find was getting farther
and farther away." I must have been giving her an
accusing look or something because she stopped
short.

"Don't get me wrong, Red. I loved Lance. At first, I
was none too thrilled to find out I was going to have
a baby. But once he was here I loved him. For himself
I loved him a whole lot. But I didn't love being somebody's mother. I still hadn't had my turn at being a
kid myself." She gave me a searching look "Can you
begin to understand what I mean, Red?"

I nodded. "Yeah, I understand what you're saying'."
I said. And that part I really did understand. I'd seen
it happen around here. Some girl gets married right
out of high school and has a baby and, for about a
year, she's a real celebrity, with all her friends hanging around her goo-gooing at the baby and envying
her being a real grown-up woman. But a year later
everything's changed. Her friends have all gone to
college or got jobs in the city. Their lives are just
beginning. But all she's got to look forward to is
spending the rest of her life doing the same old thing.
No future, as Anne-Marie said.

"I stuck it out for five years, Red. Maybe I'd have
stayed forever, but one day Jerry, the guy whose
band I used to sing with, tracked me down. He'd cut
a couple of demo records and got himself enough
publicity to line up a tour down east in some big
night clubs. If that worked out well enough he'd

have a shot at Nashville — and he wanted me to go along.''

She said that word 'Nashville' with a sort of reverence. It made me think of an article I'd once read about the Moslems making pilgrimages to the Holy City of Mecca. I think that to her going to Nashville was the same sort of thing.

Anne-Marie had got to the end of her story. There was a long silence. She lit another cigarette. I polished imaginary dust off the Lincoln's sleek, silver hood. I didn't know what to say. That whole, one-sided conversation had left me feeling like I'd just read somebody's diary — with the owner standing there watching over my shoulder while I did it. It wasn't a very comfortable feeling.

I looked over at Anne-Marie, standing there in her sixty-dollar jeans, leaning on her thirty-thousand-dollar car, and I thought she's got it all. Money, looks, talent — you name it. And then I tried to picture her as that lonely trapped little girl. A princess, accidentally born in a tar-paper shack. Someone who was too special to accept the role fate had given her. Yeah, she was special, all right. It took someone real special to make the trip from where she started to where she was now. But, slowly, I began to realize that it hadn't been a free ride. She'd paid her dues to make that trip. To climb that far, that fast, you had to travel light. And now she was finding out just how much she had left behind.

She ground out the cigarette with her boot heel and when she looked up at me again she seemed different. No longer the big Nashville star. She was a person who had made her share of mistakes. This time, when her eyes met mine, some of the fire had gone out of them. Suddenly, I realized that she was scared. Anne-Marie Charbonneau. Scared of what this red-haired kid in a nowhere town in Alberta was thinking of her. And, for a minute, I felt almost sorry for her. I wanted to tell her that it was okay. That I understood why she had gone.

Then I remembered the look in Lance's eyes the night he'd seen her on TV and I knew I couldn't tell her those things. Because what she had done to him wasn't okay. It wasn't anywhere near okay.

"So," she said in a small voice, "I guess I've told you enough to make you hate me . . ."

I shook my head. "I don't hate you," I said, and hesitated a minute before adding, "But I can see why Lance does." It was the truth, probably the most honest thing I'd ever told an adult in my life, but I couldn't believe that I'd had the nerve to say it. Then since I'd gone that far, I didn't think I had much to lose by saying the rest of what was on my mind. "You talk about how hard it was on you to have to grow up too fast. So what did you do? You turned right around and pulled the same rotten thing on your own kid. You made Lance grow up when he was five years old. How do you think he felt? You wrote him out of your life. It was your idea, not his. Now, you think you can just erase the last ten years? Just cruise into town in your Continental and whistle and he'll come running like a faithful puppy who's been waiting on the front porch all this time? You didn't learn anything from all those bad years you're so tore up about. You didn't do any better than your own parents did . . ." I ran out of words and breath at about the same time.

I thought about what I had just said. It reminded me of something I'd once read. It was mostly about child abuse, about how almost all child abusers had been abused children themselves. But, it had gone on to tell about how most parents seemed to raise their kids about the same as *they* were raised — even if they had hated their childhoods. People whose parents were divorced were more likely to get divorced themselves. Things like that. Was that the way it worked, then, I wondered. Was Mike too rough on Lance sometimes because that was the only way he had seen parents act when he was a kid? Was I going to act just like my dad when I had kids of my own? I hoped not.

Anne-Marie's voice brought me back. "You're a mouthy kid, Red," she said, and the scared look was gone from her eyes. The fire was back and she looked like she was ready to stand her ground and fight. That was when I started to respect her, a little. I guess a lot of women would have turned on the tears by now, after all the things I'd said to her. But not her. She was a fighter.

I stood there, feeling my face start to burn and not knowing what to say. Obviously, I'd said more than enough already. I figured she was going to take a strip off of me and I wouldn't have blamed her much. What she did say took me by surprise. "But, you're also an honest kid," she said, and just a hint of a smile curled the corners of her lips. "And honesty isn't easy to find these days." Then, her face went serious again. "But I don't think you understand. I'm not trying to excuse what I did. Nobody has to tell me it was a rotten thing to do. I've been telling myself every day for ten years. I'm sorry now, Red. Sorrier than you'll ever understand." Her eyes burned into me. "All I'm asking for is a chance to tell Lance I'm sorry. I still love him, Red. I need to tell him. For him, as much as for me."

I stared down at my worn runners and tried to sort out my thoughts, but my mind was running in crazy circles. "Love means never having to say you're sorry." That was a line from a real tear-jerker of a movie I saw once. I didn't remember much else about the movie but I never forgot that line — mainly because I had thought it was about the stupidest statement I had ever heard. Now, Anne-Marie was telling me just the opposite. Maybe she was right. Maybe love meant having to say you *were* sorry and travelling hundreds of miles to do it. And she might be right about something else, too. Whether Lance wanted to see her or not, talking to her, having it out with her, face to face, might be the only way he was going to get his life straightened out.

I sighed, feeling like one of those soldiers we read about in a poem in English class. Like I was charging straight into the Valley of Death but I still couldn't turn back. "Okay, what do you want me to do?" I asked miserably.

Anne-Marie should have looked relieved. She had got what she wanted. But she looked worried. And I realized just how hard it was going to be for her to face Lance after all these years. This was going to be one tense situation I was getting myself in the middle of.

"I'll be in Calgary for the next couple of weeks. Set up a meeting anywhere, anytime, and I'll be there. Just phone this number and give me a day's warning." She took a pen out of her purse and wrote a number on a scrap of paper. I took it. "Okay," I said wearily, and started walking away.

"Red!" I stopped and looked back.

"Thanks."

13

The weather stayed showery for the next few days.
It seemed like every day the sun would sit up there
beating down and turning the school into one giant
sauna — until about three o'clock. Then the storm
clouds would start rolling in and by the time I got
home it would be pouring again. It really got on my
nerves. To tell the truth, I guess everything got on
my nerves. Final exams weren't far off and even
though Dad still wasn't talking to me much I could
feel the pressure. So I worried about exams. I didn't
study or do anything useful like that. I just worried.

Lance wasn't helping matters much either. He
was still going around acting half-spaced. Like nothing he did had his full attention. It bugged me. But,
what bugged me most of all was that promise I'd
made to Anne-Marie. Looking back, I was sure that
it had been nothing short of an attack of temporary
insanity that had made me agree to setting Lance
up like that for her. But if I was going to do it, I
wanted to get it over with. I couldn't stand having it
hanging over me like a distant date with the execu-
tioner. I didn't have the faintest clue of just how I
was going to arrange this marvellous meeting — and
that wasn't improving my disposition any.

Then one night, right out of the blue, I found the perfect place — and it was even Lance's own idea to go there. We were doing math homework at his place. That is, I was doing math homework. He was already finished and now he was pacing around the room, bored and restless. He pulled back the curtain and looked outside. It was late evening and almost dark but I could see that the sky was clear all the way to where it disappeared behind the mountains. "It's not gonna rain tomorrow," he announced.

"Yeah?" I said absently, wrestling with a negative integer.

"Let's ride somewhere after school."

"Okay. Where?" A minus times a minus is a plus. Now there's a typical example of mathematical logic. Useful, too.

"The Cliffs. We haven't been there yet this year."

"Okay," I agreed again, trying unsuccessfully to factor 117. Suddenly, a little switch in my brain clicked. Not about 117. About The Cliffs. They were the place! The solution to my problem. I jumped to my feet. "All right! You're on! Right after school."

Lance gave me a funny look. I guess that much enthusiasm from me just then was kind of surprising. I didn't stick around long enough for him to get suspicious, though. I had to go home and make a phone call.

I thought it was going to take a lot of explanation for Anne-Marie to understand where to be to meet Lance tomorrow but, as soon as I said 'The Cliffs' she cut in, "Sure, I know the place."

"You do?" I said, surprised.

"Red, I lived on Silverwinds for five years," she reminded me. "It was one of my favourite places."

"Yeah?" That surprised me, too. It was one of my favourite places and I hadn't thought that Anne-Marie and I would have that much in common. Then, another thought struck me. "It's quite a ways from the road . . ." I began, wondering how she was going to get there.

She read my mind. "I'll borrow a horse," she said. "Sherrie Willmore will lend me one."

Sherrie Willmore. Mother of the infamous Gremlin twins. The Willmores lived right between Du-charmes and us. No wonder Anne-Marie knew all there was to know about Lance and me . . .

It didn't rain the next day so as soon as I got off the bus I saddled Pepper and rode over to meet Lance. It was about three miles to The Cliffs, over where the river cut, and I mean literally cut, through the far southwest corner of Silverwinds. I don't know what the geological explanation was but, for some rea-son, the river had carved itself a regular canyon there. Over the years, the canyon had widened out till it was more like a narrow valley now and the cliffs weren't so sheer any more. The banks were still steep enough, though, and with a twenty or thirty foot drop down to the river flat it wasn't the greatest place for livestock to be grazing along the edge. Frank had decided the safest thing to do was just to sacri-fice a little bit of grass and had run a fence along the top of the cliffs, a few yards back from the edge. That left just room enough for a narrow horse trail between the fence and the bank. It was a great place to ride but it was a little dangerous, too, so you had to stay awake.

There was always lots to see from there. Usually, there were a few families of bank swallows nesting in the dirt of the cliffs and if you watched the wil-lows along the river long enough you could usually spot some deer or moose browsing down there some-where.

Today, though, if there had been a purple elephant

with green ears grazing in the valley I probably would have missed him. I could hardly ride in a straight line, my mind was so wrapped up in wondering if Anne-Marie was going to show up and imagining what would happen if she did . . .

We rode as far as we could, till the west fence of the ranch met the fence along the cliff trail and stopped us. We got off there, left the horses ground-tied to graze and sat and looked down over the river valley. That is, Lance looked over the river valley. I mainly looked back along the trail we had come on, watching for another rider coming down that trail. It's funny that Lance didn't notice how nervous I was. Normally, he would have spotted something wrong in about two minutes. But, like I said, these days he wasn't concentrating.

Then, suddenly, both our horses looked up and turned their heads toward the east. Lance and I both saw her at about the same time. There she was. Anne-Marie, riding a pinto horse and coming down the trail at an easy lope, still too far away to recognize.

"Hey, who is that?" Lance said, standing up to get a better look.

I stood up, too, and tried to decide what to say. I had three choices. Lie, tell the truth, or play dumb. Either of the first two was going to get me in trouble, sooner or later, so I decided to just act natural and go for number three. I shrugged and mumbled something that made no sense.

It was at about that moment when it occurred to me that the time had come for me to get out of there. The deal had been for me to get them together. It didn't include being there to referee when they met. Inconspicuously, I edged toward my horse. Just as I swung into the saddle Lance turned toward me. "Yeah, let's go see who it is," he said, getting on his horse, too. I gulped. This wasn't exactly what I'd had in mind.

He put Spider into a lope and headed down the trail, toward Anne-Marie. Well, there was no other way out of that place so I didn't have much choice. I followed.

Seconds later Lance reined in so hard that Pepper almost stepped on Spider's heels. Spider flattened his ears and gave her a warning look over his shoulder. She swerved and came up beside him, crowding close in the narrow space.

One look at Lance's face was enough to tell me — he knew. Anne-Marie was close enough now he could hardly not recognize her. Lance had gone white. He sat there staring, frozen. Spider tossed his head and pranced nervously, wanting to get going. Lance stopped him with a vicious jerk that almost set the horse back on his haunches. I'd known this was going to be a bad scene but that was the first time I fully understood the effect Anne-Marie had on Lance. In the time he'd been riding Spider, I'd seen the horse half-kill Lance a dozen times but he had never once done anything to hurt that horse. And now, one look at Anne-Marie and he practically breaks Spider's neck . . .

I was getting out of there. I started to ease Pepper past him. But I didn't do it fast enough. Lance caught my movement out of the corner of his eye. His hand shot out and grabbed my rein. Slowly his eyes left Anne-Marie and turned to focus on me. Two laser beams. Cold fire that etched into me like acid. "You knew," he whispered. "You set it all up . . ." I'd heard snakes with less venom in their voices. I knew he was going to drag me off my horse right there and probably beat my brains out. And, in that moment, I didn't really care. Anybody as stupid as I had been didn't have much to lose in that department . . .

But before either of us could make a move, Anne-Marie's voice rang out. "Lance!" she called. We both turned to look. She had reined in about forty feet down the trail and was sitting there, holding her fidgeting horse in check. She rode like she had been born to it.

"Lance, I want to talk to you. Just the two of us," she said, her voice calm.

I was watching Lance all the time, trying to read his expression. But that was impossible. It was like a newspaper page that had been accidentally double-printed. Too many emotions, all blurred together. One thing for sure, though — happiness wasn't among them.

I could hear Lance breathing. He sounded like he had run a long way. He didn't answer for a minute. Then he swallowed hard, like he was trying to get his voice under control. He didn't manage it, though. "No!" he said, and he sounded like he was going to choke on the word. "No. I got nothin' to say to you."

"Then just listen to me. Come on, Lance, give me a break. Please. Just five minutes. There are some things I really need to tell you . . ." Her voice was pleading, but not in a weak, helpless kind of way. In a way that showed how bad she wanted to talk to him — and how hard she'd fight to make him give in.

I could almost feel him wavering. He dropped my bridle rein and wiped his hand across his eyes. I heard something halfway between a deep breath and a sob. He looked up and faced her dead on.

"You don't have five minutes," he said, his voice rising. "You're already way too late."

"Late?" her voice was puzzled. "I don't understand . . ."

"Nine years and seven months late. Now get outa my way. Get outa my life!"

He nudged Spider into a walk. But Anne-Marie stopped him. "No. I won't get out of your life. I tried that once and I've regretted it ever since. You might just as well settle down and stop having tantrums and listen to me, Lance. Because I'm not letting you out of here until —"

Suddenly Lance's eyes blazed. "Yeah? Well you just try and stop me, lady!" He dug his heels into Spider's ribs and the horse gave a leap that sent a spray of dirt flying up behind his hoofs. He charged straight toward where Anne-Marie was sitting with the pinto turned sideways, deliberately blocking the narrow trail. Lance was going to call her bluff. But Anne-Marie wasn't bluffing. She held her horse steady and sat there, head up, the fire in her eyes answering his.

Lance wasn't bluffing either. The distance between them was narrowing. I couldn't believe it — two of a kind, out here playing chicken on horseback . . .

Then, with what looked like only inches left between them, Lance suddenly reined hard to the left. Spider obeyed instantly with the quickness of a natural born cow-horse and I watched, horrified, as horse and rider disappeared over the edge of the bank.

I stopped breathing. I couldn't believe what my eyes had just seen. Hardly realizing I had moved, I found myself inching Pepper as close to the crumbling edge as I dared. I sensed more than saw Anne-Marie beside me . . .

I stared down that bank — thirty or forty feet of crumbly clay and gravel, held together with the odd scraggly clump of bunchgrass. Not really a cliff — but a bank I'd think twice before I climbed down — on foot, I mean.

The only other time I'd ever seen anybody ride down a bank that steep was in some Australian western that made a big hit over here. I remembered that Lance and I had got in a big argument with some of the other kids at school. They had thought it was great. We had thought it had been the phoniest thing since Boy George's eyelashes. Nobody could have ridden down a slope that steep, I didn't think.

But the scene I was watching now wasn't phony. It was so real it terrified me. Lance was going to kill himself . . . At first, I couldn't see anything but dust down there. And I didn't want to see. I was sure that, when the dust cleared, Lance and Spider would be piled up on the river flat — both with their necks broken.

Then, almost at the bottom, I caught a glimpse of something fire-red. Spider. Still on his feet. Still moving. Jumpsliding down that slope, loose dirt and pebbles following in a miniature avalanche behind him. And Lance was still in the saddle. Balanced like an arrow on a bow, every muscle taut, his body so much in time with Spider's that he was like a part of the horse, moving with him — leaning, holding, balancing. The two of them, turned into a Centaur and defying gravity. Defying the whole world.

They were at the bottom. Lance reined Spider in on the sandy flat and I could see him lean out of the saddle, first on one side, then on the other. Checking the horse's legs, looking at the way he stood, looking for injuries. Then he must have been satisfied that the horse was okay, because he sat up straight in the saddle and looked up. Up to where Anne-Marie and I sat, frozen on our horses at the edge of the bank. He didn't wave or call to us. He just looked at us for a few seconds. He was too far away for me to see his face . . .

Suddenly he leaned forward low on Spider's neck, and they were gone. A red flame racing along the river like a fire following a trail of gunpowder. A minute later they rounded a bend and disappeared from sight.

Slowly, my mind began to thaw itself out. Pepper tossed her head and whinnied, impatiently. I looked down at my hand on the reins. My knuckles were white. I loosened my grip. I felt winded. Like I'd been in a long race — or held my breath a long time. I took a few deep breaths before I remembered. Anne-Marie.

I looked over at her. She hadn't moved. She was staring into the distance, her eyes on the bend where Lance had ridden out of sight. I expected her to be upset — scared, hurt, maybe just plain mad. But when she turned so I could see her face I realized I was wrong. Oh, maybe there were some of those emotions there someplace but, if they were, they were having to take second place. Because the only way I could have described what I saw on her face right then was pride, pride and admiration. She shook her head. "Wow," she said softly. "He's quite a kid."

That was all she said. Someone else might feel proud if their kid made the basketball team or got straight As or something, but Anne-Marie wasn't your average mother. She was proud because her kid risked breaking his neck to prove a point. And the funny part was, I could understand why she felt that way.

Then another thing struck me. She wasn't surprised. Maybe shocked a little at the moment he plunged down the bank, but not really long-term surprised that he could do something that wild. "You knew how he'd react when you met, didn't you?" I asked accusingly.

She smiled. "I didn't think it would be quite this extreme."

"But it didn't exactly blow your mind when it happened, did it?"

She shook her head. "No, it's just the sort of thing I would have done at his age."

14

When I'd left Anne-Marie there at The Cliffs I knew that her big scheme to get together with Lance had succeeded at only one thing — messing up my friendship with him. But it wasn't until the next morning that I realized just how bad it was messed up.

When Lance got on the bus I picked my books up off the seat and made room for him, just like usual. But he didn't sit down. He didn't say a word. He just gave me a look that would have made a snake shiver and kept on walking down the aisle. He sat down behind me, in the seat where Johnny Hammer would have been if he hadn't been at home with the mumps. I turned around. I was going to get things straightened out with Lance. This was getting really ridiculous.

But he turned away and was staring out the window, his face blank, his eyes empty, I gave up temporarily. There was no use trying to talk to him when he was like that. He'd get over it, I told myself.

But he didn't get over it. He didn't talk to me at all for the next four days. I counted them. After that, he loosened up to the point where he said things like, "Here," when he passed me the basketball in Phys. Ed. Not exactly heart-to-heart talk. I was hardly seeing enough of him to talk anyway. He hadn't been coming home on the bus in the afternoons lately, which was pretty strange for him. I didn't know what he was up to. Then, one afternoon, a streak of white whistled past the bus and squealed through the Silverwinds gate. That's when I caught on. Lance was getting a ride home with Randy every day. And I began to wonder why.

Maybe he was spending his noon hours cruising with Randy too. That would explain why I'd thought I caught a whiff of pot drifting into class with Lance a couple of times. It was from riding around in Randy's car — I hoped.

After school the next day we were both at our locker — he hadn't managed to get his locker changed, yet.

"You goin' home on the bus tonight?" I asked, trying to sound casual, to get us back being friends without having to make a big deal out of it.

Lance didn't even look at me. "No, Randy's givin' me a ride," he said, and started to walk off.

"Randy!" I burst out, forgetting to be casual. "What is this with you and Randy hanging out together? Randy's a jerk."

Lance threw me one backward glance as he walked away. "Randy's a cool guy," he said. "He doesn't mess around with other people's lives."

Yeah, great. Randy doesn't mess around with other people's lives, but I do, right? Just that once I'd got involved where I didn't belong and it looked like Lance was going to hold it against me forever.

I thought about that all the way home, and while I did my chores, and it was still on my mind when I finished eating. I kept thinking about it as I saddled Pepper and headed out to the road. It wasn't until I had turned her towards Silverwinds that I really understood what I was going to do. I was going down there. I was going to talk to Lance whether he liked it or not. Have it all out with him, once and for all. I nudged Pepper into a lope.

I had turned into the lane and was halfway to Ducharme's house before I noticed it, parked there in the shadows of the yard. The big, silver Continental.

I turned Pepper so fast that she pivoted a hundred and eighty degrees on her hind legs. We went home at a dead gallop.

What had Anne-Marie been doing at the house?

It didn't look like I was going to find out. I wasn't about to get in any more conversations with her if my life depended on it and I sure couldn't ask Lance.

If he'd been kind of spacey before, now he was totally freaked out. He was skipping classes, flunking easy tests, hanging around with every creep in the school. And he treated me like I was dead. He didn't act mad at me any more. He just acted like I didn't exist. He acted like his schoolwork didn't exist either. I could tell the teachers were beginning to wonder what was wrong with him, too. It was only going to be a matter of time before one of them tangled with him if he didn't quit sitting there in class like some kind of a zombie.

It finally happened in social studies period. Mr. Montrose was delivering one of his lectures — that's what he called them, lectures. What that meant was he talked and we were supposed to make notes on the parts that we thought were important — which was probably why nobody took many notes in his class.

Actually, I think Montrose must have been some kind of a frustrated university professor who had somehow got stuck with a job in a junior high. And junior high got stuck with him, too. He gave new meaning to the word 'boring.'

He never said anything in two words if he could

find a way to say it in twenty. And a good percentage of those words were usually about himself — a subject he obviously found fascinating. At least a dozen times this year he had told us all about his ancestors. He could trace them back to the United Empire Loyalists, a fact which he apparently thought should impress somebody. It didn't impress me. If he could have traced his ancestry back to Tarzan's pet chimp, it wouldn't have impressed me either — but I might have been able to see a family resemblance. Bloodlines might matter when it came to buying a horse but I didn't figure that they made much difference with people.

Anyhow, today he spared us the ancestors. He was talking about the Riel Rebellion — which could have been one of the few halfway interesting events in Canadian history. But not the way *he* told it. It takes real talent to make a rebellion dull, but Montrose managed it. Ten minutes into the period, the whole class had taken up its normal boredom-survival activities. Sandi McKenzie was reading a movie magazine inside her notebook, Barb Johanneson was doing something to her fingernails, Dave Schneider was finishing his math — and I was taking a mental survey of what everyone was doing.

Normally Lance and I would have been carrying on a silent conversation across the room. We had almost perfected the art of lip-reading since Montrose had moved us as far apart as he could, back in September.

But today Lance wasn't talking to me. I looked over at him to see what he was doing. He was slumped down in his desk like he was half asleep. But I could see that he had his pen in his hand. For one crazy second I thought that he was actually taking notes. I leaned back in my desk so I could see him better. No, he wasn't taking notes — not unless he was writing them on his hand. Then he moved a little and I got a good look at what he was doing. Drawing rock group logos on the back of his hand. He had already finished IRON MAIDEN. I could read those big, black letters across the room. His hand looked just like an album cover. Now he had his red pen out. (Mr. Montrose had made us all buy red pens "to mark important things." I wondered if this would fit his idea of important.)

I watched as Lance did S C O R . . . Scorpions, this one was going to be. I wondered when Lance had developed this sudden love for Heavy Metal music.

I never got to finish wondering, because right then Mr. Montrose also happened to notice what Lance was doing. He stopped talking, right in mid-sentence, and stared at Lance, giving him one of those teacher-looks that are supposed to turn the victim into a mass of quivering jelly. Lance didn't look up. That really frosted Montrose. How can you destroy some-one with your "killer look" if he doesn't even know he's being looked at? He flung his notes on the table and strode down the aisle to Lance's desk. Slowly Lance looked up at him.

"Am I interrupting something?" Montrose asked, in his most sarcastic voice. Lance didn't say a word; he just kept his steady gaze on Montrose.

The teacher's voice rose a notch, and some of the other kids started to watch with interest. "Just exact-ly what do you think you're doing?"

"Nothin' ," Lance said, softly.

"Nothing! Yes that is just what you're doing, and what you have been doing for the last week. There have been three assignments due in the last few days and you have handed none of them in. Do you realize what that does to your year's mark? If you're not careful you're going to manage to fail this sub-ject." He was really yelling now but when Lance answered it was still in that low, distant-sounding voice.

"I don't care," he said. Quiet as those words came out, everyone in the class heard them. It was dead silent now, and everyone was listening. I could feel my hands sweating.

Montrose acted like he hadn't heard, though. He went on as if Lance hadn't said anything. "And you, of all people, should be listening to today's lesson. Louis Riel was one of the heroes of the Métis people, a great leader, although a misguided one. Aren't you even interested in your own history?"

"I don't care," Lance said again, but this time his voice was beginning to take on an edge that showed he did care — a lot.

Mr. Montrose threw up his hands, grandstanding for the class now. It was probably the first time in history he had been able to get their undivided attention. "You don't care!" he repeated. "That is exactly the point I am trying to make. It is that kind of uncaring attitude that has plagued your people throughout their history, a history of apathy and ignorance. And now *you* sit here with every opportunity before you, with the intelligence to break out of the mould, to *make* something of yourself, and the only thing you can say is that you don't care. Is that to be your destiny then, to repeat the same mistakes that your people have always made? The same sort of mistakes that caused them to lose their land and that led to this part of history that you don't care about?"

I couldn't believe what I was hearing. Stop it, Montrose, I was screaming silently. Don't push him any farther. Quit while you've both still got the chance to back off. Most animals will run before they'll fight — unless they're cornered. And I didn't think people were much different. Right now, Lance was hurting from things that Montrose couldn't begin to understand and all he wanted was to be left alone. But Montrose had to pick today to get on his case. And to start in on him about being part Indian . . .

I'd never known Lance to have any hang-ups about being part Indian. In fact, generally he was proud of it and I knew the rest of us envied him more than looked down on him — there was at least one person who would have traded red hair and sunburn for Lance's kind of dark good looks.

It was Lance who had started the "Paleface" routine with me, and when I'd automatically thrown the "Geronimo" label back at him, he had thought it was great. We'd been calling each other those names for a long time now.

And he'd told me some neat stuff about his ancestors. Like, way back somewhere, his dad's great-grandfather, I think, was a famous chief. A great leader. War Lance was his name, and that was who Lance had been named after. I had never thought of Lance being as much an Indian name as a white one but that was pretty cool, having a name that fit in both worlds. It suited Lance, too, because he seemed to have ended up with the best of both backgrounds.

There had only been one time that I'd ever seen him get hassled over being part Indian. Some new kid had moved in from down east last year and I guess he'd decided he was going to be Mr. King Hood in little old Alderton. And for some reason he had picked Lance as the guy to beat to make himself a reputation. So right from the start, he was needling Lance. But Lance wasn't easy to needle. Mostly he just ignored the guy or laughed at him — until the day the guy called him a stupid half-breed. The look in Lance's eyes went pure tiger then, and he landed all over that kid. It was the most famous fight of the year — and the shortest. Mr. Philipchuk, our new science teacher, was on supervision that day and he saw the whole thing, including what started it. He just stood there and watched — until he was sure that Lance had beat the daylights out of that kid. Then, he came "hurrying" over and broke it up.

A lot of us learned a whole new respect for Mr. Philipchuk that day. And the new kid learned something too. Lance could call himself a half-breed — which I'd heard him do lots of times. And his friends might even get away with it. But whoever called him that had better do it with a smile — and they'd better not add adjectives . . .

Lance slowly stood up to face Montrose and, for the second time since I'd known him, I saw that "tiger" look.

"They didn't *lose* their land," he said, and his voice was still low, but now it had an edge that cut like a knife. "It was stolen from them." He paused for a second and then added, "And it was people like your tenth generation pedigreed ancestors who stole it."

Mr. Montrose's face went white. He was furious. "All right," he said in a taut voice. "This has gone far enough. You're coming down to the office." Then he reached out and grabbed Lance by the arm. And even across the room, I could see Lance's whole body go rigid.

Suddenly, the air in that room was dead still. I saw Lance's hands clench into fists. Oh, God, don't let Lance hit him. And don't let him hit Lance. Because, if he did, I *knew* that Lance would hit him back.

And get kicked out of school, suspended at the very least. And when you got suspended in our school, you had to fight to get back in. It all got real political. I knew of kids who'd been kicked out for stuff serious enough that I thought they'd never get back. But they did because their parents had the nerve to raise a stink all the way to the Department of Education.

But Mike Ducharme would never even fight the

County Board of Education. I doubted that he would as much as come to see Mr. Schafer at school.

Mike cared as much about Lance as any of those parents cared about their kids, probably a lot more than some of them, but that didn't make any difference. School was just too far out of his territory. Lance said all those educated people made him feel ignorant, and nothing anybody could say would change that feeling. I could have told him that ignorance was no stranger to educated people. After all, Montrose had an MEd behind his name . . .

Let it go, Lance, I wanted to yell. Let it go and just walk away. You've got reason enough to hit him, but you can knock him into the middle of next year and you're still gonna lose.

But I couldn't say a word. It was just between the two of them, one on one. All I could do was sit there staring at them and drowning in guilt. Maybe if I hadn't got mixed up in something that was none of my business, Lance wouldn't have come to school so strung-out that all Montrose had to do to push him over the edge was be his usual stupid self.

I've never been sure if I believe in stuff like mental telepathy, but that day I almost think it might have been working. Because, even though I didn't make a sound, Lance turned ever so slightly. His eyes left Mr. Montrose's face and just for a second they came to rest on mine. All I could do was meet that look and shake my head. Maybe it was enough. Or maybe it didn't make any difference. Maybe Lance had just had enough time to get in control again. I guess I'll never know why for sure, but for whatever reason, he relaxed a little. I could see him start to breathe again.

With one violent movement, he jerked his arm free. "I can find the office all by myself," he said. "Don't worry I won't get lost. *My people* are real good at following trails."

He turned, and then he was gone. The slamming of the door filled the silence that he left behind. Mr. Montrose stood there, stunned, staring at the rest of us for a few seconds. Then, he stormed out to the office.

Lance didn't show up in any classes for the rest of the day. And, for all I learned, I might as well not have been there either. I made half a dozen excuses to go by the office, hoping that Lance would be sitting on the bench and I'd get a chance to talk to him. But he was never there.

On about my sixth trip, Mrs. Kreswell took pity on me. She looked up from her typing and nodded toward Mr. Schafer's closed door. "He's been in there all afternoon," she said, and went back to her work.

Lance didn't get on the bus after school either. But, when Randy Borowski's car peeled through the parking lot just as we were pulling out, Lance was in the passenger's seat.

I heard later, through the trusty school grapevine, that Mr. Schafer had strapped Lance. Personally, I thought that he'd picked the wrong guy to beat. If anybody had it coming, it was Montrose. Still, things could have been worse. At least Lance didn't get suspended. And physical punishment didn't faze him too much. One thing for sure, when it came to laying on a licking, Mr. Schafer couldn't hold a candle to Mike Ducharme.

I also found out later that Montrose didn't exactly come out smelling like a rose. (The pun is strictly accidental.) Bobbi-Jo Carson told me that Mr. Schafer had interviewed her and some other kids about what had happened.

Bobbi-Jo lives out near us and practises her barrel-racing horse in the Silverwinds arena quite a bit and sometimes she goes riding with Lance and me. She was on the Honour Roll and had a reputation around school for being reliable so I suppose Mr. Schafer thought she would give him the story straight. I thought she would too. And she sure wouldn't pull any punches to protect Montrose, especially not when it had anything to do with Lance. I mean, pretty soon she was going to have the most over-trained horse in Alberta — or some of those trips to Silverwinds had more to do with seeing Lance than using the arena . . .

I wished that somebody would have interviewed me. I sure could have told them what happened. But I guess nobody thought I was the best source of unprejudiced opinion, considering how close Lance and I were — had been, I mean.

Anyway, Mr. Montrose was fairly subdued the next day. He didn't lecture at all. He just told us to read the next chapter and answer the questions at the end. And he made it a point never to look at Lance.

Lance looked at him, though. Stared at him all period. Like a wolf I'd seen once on holidays, when we'd stopped at one of those two-bit roadside zoos. The wolf had been chained to a tree and all the time we were there, it never moved. Just lay there, watching and waiting.

15

The next day got off to a bad start. The phone woke me up about 6:00 a.m. It was Mom talking on it. She sounded worried. By the time I got up and dressed she was in her bedroom, packing her suitcase. The phone call had been from her mother, out in Victoria. My grandfather had just been rushed to the hospital with a heart attack. The doctor had told them it wasn't critical, but Mom was taking the next plane she could get out of Calgary. She didn't know how long she'd be gone.

Before she even walked out the door I missed her. Mostly, I guess I missed having her there as sort of a netural party between Dad and me. We were going to have a great time alone together — almost as much fun as a good case of whooping cough. I was worried about Grandpa, too. I wasn't so sure there was any such thing as an uncritical heart attack.

I was depressed even before I got to school. Then, right in first period, I got called to the office. Specifically to Cassidy's office.

All the way down the hall I tried to figure out what I had done this time. My marks were okay — better than usual, in fact. The last while, since Lance and I weren't hanging around together, life had been so boring that I'd actually been doing extra homework. And, for the same reason, I'd been behaving myself in class, too.

Mrs. Kreswell told me to go right in. No waiting? I didn't know if that was a good omen or a bad one. Miss Cassidy looked up as I opened the door. She looked real serious. "Sit down, Red," she said. Red? Maybe I wasn't in too much trouble after all. I sat down.

She didn't say anything for a long time, just sat there with that worried look on her face. And that started me worrying again. Whatever I had done must have been real bad. Cassidy isn't usually stuck for words. In fact I could remember one time in my first few months in Alderton High when she'd yelled at me for nearly half an hour, steady. It made enough of an impression on me that I still haven't forgotten some of the things she said. It was the biggest fight I'd ever had with a teacher and it had all happened because I'd failed an important test by not doing one real long question that seemed like it would be just too much work. I wasn't the only one with that idea. At least a dozen kids didn't do that question but I was the one that got hauled in on the carpet.

"It's not fair!" I'd yelled, dimly realizing that I was mouthing off to a teacher, but too mad to care. "I wasn't the only one that failed that stupid test. But I'm the one who gets picked on." — my voice sounded like I was going to start bawling.

"Picked on? Sure you get picked on, and if you weren't so busy snivelling about it you might realize why you get picked on. You get picked on because you just might turn out to be worth the trouble. What you'd better start worrying about is what'll happen if I, and a lot of other people, stop taking the trouble to pick on you."

With that, Cassidy had stalked out of the room

and left me sitting there, too stunned to get up and leave. No teacher had ever talked to me like that before. By all the rules in my book, I should have hated her after that. But I didn't. I didn't hate her at all. From then on, Cassidy was my favourite teacher — but I'd still rather walk through fire than to get her that mad at me again.

She must have read my mind. "Relax, Red. You didn't do anything this time. Or . . ." and she smiled, "if you did, I haven't found out about it yet." Then her face turned serious again and, out of the blue, she came up with the question. "Red, what's wrong with Lance?"

It was the last thing I was expecting and I didn't know what to say. Then I realized that even if I'd been given a week to rehearse I still wouldn't have known what to say.

She misread my silence. "Sorry," she said. "I guess I had no right to ask you that question. Look, I don't want you to betray any confidences. Lance's personal problems aren't the school's business unless he chooses to make them so. But I want you to get the ground rules of this conversation straight. This isn't one of those cases of 'kids against the teachers so don't talk even if they torture you.' Lance isn't in any trouble with me. Or with Mr. Schafer, for that matter. He got the strap for that little performance in social class because he didn't leave Mr. Schafer any choice. Mr. Schafer gave Lance every opportunity to explain his reasons for exploding the way he did but he refused to say anything. Mr. Schafer could hardly pat him on the head for defying a teacher just because it seemed like a good idea at the time."

She got up and walked over to the window and stood looking out. Then, abruptly, she changed the subject. Or at least she seemed to. It was a couple of minutes later when I realized it was actually still the same subject. "I see a lot of kids in this job," she said. "And they're all different. Some of them are the born winners — good homes, good parents. Nothing the system does for them — or to them — is going to make much difference. They'll still come out on top.

"Then, there are the ones that have it all going for them, all the background and support in the world — but they still don't make it because they just don't have enough backbone to use what they've got going for them. Those," she said harshly, "I'd like to kick into the middle of next year.

"And there are the born losers. Three strikes against them before they ever get to school. There's just too much bad home life to overcome. You can break your heart trying to help them but they're still losers.

"But, just once in a while, you find a kid who starts out with the odds stacked against him. One who, by all the rules, should turn out to be a loser — but who isn't. Because he's a special enough person to beat the odds, to make it anyway . . ."

She turned to face me again. "I really thought Lance was going to make it," she said. Then, I understood how all the things she had said were tied together. And I remembered how I had thought that same word after I had talked to Anne-Marie the first time. Special. Maybe being special was the worst thing that could happen to you. It seemed like everyone had always thought that my brother, Greg, was a pretty special person . . .

Miss Cassidy was still talking, " . . .but now, all of a sudden, he's changed. It's not just this incident with Mr. Montrose. There's a lot more to it than that. It's his whole attitude — I gather he's been not handing work in, skipping classes, hanging around with some pretty unclassy people . . .But," she interrupted herself, "I'm not telling you anything you don't already know, am I, Red?"

She gave me a long look, one that was hard to meet. I bent over to retie my runner and shook my head.

"What are we going to do, Red?" She sounded tired.

We? I didn't know what she was going to do but my half of we had already done more than enough. I was going to mind my own business and try not to mess things up any worse.

"Did you talk to him?" I asked. Guidance was her job, not mine.

She smiled wearily and shook her head. "No, I talked at him. He spent twenty minutes in here yesterday, staring at that floor tile in front of you. I could have got more answers by talking to the wall."

She sighed and sat down again. "He's heading for trouble, Red. Something's got him so messed up that he doesn't know what he's doing. But one thing's for sure. Nobody can keep that kind of pressure bottled up inside forever. One of these days he's going to blow and, well, Lance is a tough kid but I'm not sure he's going to be tough enough to survive that kind of an explosion."

She sat there silent for a minute, toying with the empty coffee cup that had joined the rest of the stuff on her desk. Then she added, "If there was some way that I could follow him around and stop that explosion from happening, I'd do it. But I'm an adult — and a teacher. And those are two strikes against me getting anywhere near him these days."

She stopped talking and sat looking at me until I couldn't stall any longer. I had to look up at her.

"How come you're telling me all this? What am I supposed to do about it?" I asked it half-defiantly because I was afraid that I already knew the answer

—and I didn't like it. I was going to end up caught in the middle again. Just like I had been with Greg. Caught in the middle and feeling guilty. Because I had seen it coming and hadn't done anything to stop it.

Miss Cassidy shook her head. "I don't know, Red. I don't know what you're supposed to do any more than I know what I'm supposed to do. Being his friend in the next while is going to be hard — no, probably close to impossible. But just don't write him off. However much it may seem like that's what he wants you to do, believe me, it isn't. Eventually Lance is going to need you. And when that time comes, Red, be there."

I knew she was right. I guess I'd been thinking the same thing somewhere in the back of my mind all along. But I still wished she hadn't said it. Maybe then I could have pushed it out of my mind. Maybe I still could — but I didn't think so.

I sighed and stood up. "Okay," I said tiredly. "I'll try."

Miss Cassidy stood up, too. "Thanks, Red," she said. I turned to open the door but she stopped me. "He's worth it," she said, and gave me a long, level look. I understood what she meant. Lance wasn't the first mixed-up kid she'd thought was worth fighting for.

I grinned. "Yeah," I said. "I know." I started to open the door but a thought struck me and I stopped. "Oh, there's one more thing I should tell you," I said seriously.

She came over to the door. "What is it?" she asked.

"Well, I don't quite know how to tell you this, but . . ."

"But what?" she said, starting to sound worried.

"But we tried your advice. And there's no way you'll ever catch trout with dew worms."

"There's no way you'll what?" she began, and then started to laugh.

I was laughing, too. And mentally chalking up a point. It wasn't very often that I got one on Cassidy.

"Get out of here, you red-headed turkey!" she said, and messed up my hair before I could make it through the door.

I was still laughing as I walked back to class. Cassidy had laid some heavy stuff on me but I was still feeling better than I had for a long time. Just knowing there was someone else around who understood helped a lot.

16

I read once that it's the little things that change the course of history. Like some general's horse had a shoe that wasn't nailed on right and the shoe came off in the middle of a battle so the horse fell and the general was killed and the war was lost — all because of a horseshoe nail. Well, on June 12, it was a sliver in the chalkboard ledge that changed history for me — and Lance.

It was just before afternoon break and Mrs. Miller was teaching us English. She dropped her chalk and went to slide between the ledge and the filing cabinet to pick up a new piece. The space was kind of narrow, a little narrower than Mrs. Miller, I think. Anyway, she suddenly let out a squawk. That ledge was splintery and she'd got a big sliver right in her . . . hip. I guess that wasn't the first time she'd been assaulted by that ledge because she freaked right out, stopped everything right in the middle of the prepositional phrase and sent a kid to the industrial arts room for a piece of sandpaper.

She gave that ledge such a working over it would never bite again and then she sent me to take back what was left of the sandpaper. To get to industrial arts, you have to go out the back door of the school and into another building. Of course, I forgot that if you don't stick a shoe or something in that back door it automatically locks when you go out. Sure enough, when I came back it was locked. Gee, that was too bad. Now I'd have to walk all the way around the outside of the school to the main entrance, and by then English period would be over and I never would find out about the prepositional phrase. I didn't rush. In fact I took the long way around, past the storage area outside the gym. And that's where I ran into Lance.

I didn't actually run into him. He didn't even know I was there. I came around the corner and saw him standing there. He had his back to me but it was him all right. I knew he was skipping out. He'd been at school in the morning but he hadn't shown up for English. I hadn't thought much about it. Skipping had become a pretty regular occurrence with him lately. Still I was surprised to see him hanging around the school grounds. I was even more surprised to see who he was with. Don Watson. The prime burn-out of the whole school. Two weeks ago, Lance would never have given Watson the time of day. But as the scene in front of me registered, I realized that Lance was giving — no, selling — Watson a lot more than the time of day. Watson was studying a small, foil-wrapped package. I'd seen packages like that before. Greg used to have lots of them. I felt myself go cold.

"That's a lot of money," Watson said. "It better be good stuff."

Lance shrugged, "You don't like it, take it up with Randy. He says it's good stuff." Lance sounded as bored with this as he did with everything else these days.

Randy? Randy Borowski. Suddenly, everything clicked into place. All the time Lance had been spending with Randy . . .

I couldn't believe it. I didn't want to believe it. But I was seeing it happen. Lance was dealing for Randy.

Watson looked up then and that's when he saw me, still standing there, too shocked to move. "Hey, man, what's he doin' here?" he squawked, like a panic-stricken chicken.

Lance spun around to face me and I got the weirdest feeling that I was seeing a stranger for the first time. He'd lost a lot of weight in the last couple of weeks and his face had sort of a gaunt, haunted look. His hair hung in his eyes and curled over the collar of the black leather jacket he was wearing over a tattered Motley Crüe sweatshirt. I guess he hadn't really changed that much, just overnight, but when you're friends with someone you always see them as the same old guy, a good guy. But the way I was seeing him now, Lance didn't look like a good guy. He looked like a hood.

Of all the things about him, though, it was his eyes I noticed most. For just a second something that might have been shame flickered through them and his gaze dropped to the ground. Then he looked up again and that expression was gone. His eyes were ice-cold now, and I felt like he was looking right through me. "So, now you know, Cantrell," he said defiantly. "What you gonna do about it? Narc to your old man so he can come and arrest us? Yeah, why don't you call him and all the rest of the pigs. Let them get their brownie points for bustin' a couple of kids."

The words didn't shock me that much. When your dad's a cop you get used to garbage like that. I'd been taking it all my life. But not from Lance. Never from Lance. Not from the one guy who had always understood . . .

Somewhere, way in the back of my mind, I was remembering what Cassidy had said. That it was going to be hard to be Lance's friend. Well, she was right. But she had underestimated how hard. I was tired of caring about how he felt. Right now, I cared about how *I* felt. And I was feeling like I'd just been kicked in the face by my best friend — make that ex-best friend — make it ex-friend, period.

I wanted to yell back at him, swear at him, call him names — do something to let out the pain that was squeezing my throat so hard I couldn't swallow. But I couldn't say anything. One word right then and I would have been bawling.

So I hit him square in the mouth as hard as I could. I swung at him and the bell rang for afternoon break, right on cue, just like it was the starting signal for the big fight in a movie.

He staggered back but he didn't go down. He just stood there, with a thin trickle of blood coming from his lip, staring at me with this shocked look on his face. He hadn't believed I'd really do it. I hadn't either. But I'd wanted to hurt him. Hurt him as much as he'd hurt me. And even hitting him hadn't helped much. I hadn't even knocked him down.

I started talking then. The words just started to pour out without me even thinking about what I was saying. I couldn't have been thinking or I never would have said what I did.

"You shut up about my dad, Ducharme!" I yelled in a hoarse voice I hardly recognized. "You got no room to talk about anybody's parents . . ."

By now I was dimly aware that a crowd had gathered around. I wasn't surprised. People are a lot like sharks; a hint of blood in the air and they home in on it like they've got radar. I hated them all for standing there, taking it all in like it was the latest instalment of *The Young and the Restless* or something. But even the crowd wasn't enough to stop me from finishing what I had to say. "At least my parents both cared enough to stay around and see me grow up. That's more than you can say for your old lady."

From the look that crossed his face, I knew those words hit Lance a lot harder than my punch had. Instantly I regretted saying them. But it was too late for regrets because Lance's fist exploded against my cheek like a cannonball. The force of it threw me backward and, the next thing I knew, I was on the ground.

This was it, then? Lance and I were going to go after each other for real? I wondered why I didn't get up and light into him with both fists. I don't have this red hair for nothing and, if it had been anyone else standing there looking down at me, I wouldn't have hesitated. I had thrown that first punch fast enough. But then I realized that in spite of everything that had happened between us I couldn't fight Lance. We'd already torn each other up some, both physically and emotionally, and it seemed like we'd gone too far to stop now. I was mad enough to hit him again. But the memories kept getting in the way. Two years is a long time. Two years of being best friends. Two years of trusting each other. Fighting Lance would be too much like fighting myself. I could feel the anger beginning to drain out of me.

I looked up at Lance, standing over me, his fists still clenched, his face unreadable. Our eyes met. And suddenly I knew. He didn't want to fight me either. If we did fight, it wouldn't be for us, it would be for them. For all the people who were standing around waiting to see which one of us came out on top. It reminded me of a movie I had seen once. Ancient Rome. The gladiators, fighting and killing each other, for no better reason than that the crowd demanded blood. Yeah, civilization has come a long way . . .

Seconds hung in the air like drops of water on slowly melting icicles. The spectators were getting restless. Don Watson was there in the front row. He made me think of a hyena slinking around the edges of a lion kill, too chicken to get right into the action, but not wanting to miss anything. "Come on, Ducharme," he yelled. "You can take him. What are you waiting for? Beat his face in!"

I heard Lance take a deep breath. Then he swung around to face Watson. "Shut up, Watson," he said in a low, dangerous voice. "Just shut that stinkin' mouth of yours. You want a fight so much, get over here. I'll give you all the fight you can handle. Otherwise, get outa here!" His eyes swept the crowd. "And that goes for the rest of you, too. This ain't your fight. It ain't any of your business. So get outa here, all of you. Split!"

Instant silence. A few kids shuffled their feet nervously. Some, around the edges, started to drift away. But most just stood there, studying their shoelaces or checking their fingernails. Nobody wanted to be there any more but they didn't want to draw attention to themselves by walking away. Nobody looked at Lance.

Then the bell rang, and I could almost feel the relief that swept through that crowd and melted it away the way a chinook goes through a snowdrift. In twos and threes, they turned away and moved off toward the school.

That left Lance and me. I was still sitting on the ground like a fool. My cheek was stinging but that was nothing compared to the way the rest of my life felt. Lance stood there, watching the crowd slink away. Suddenly I noticed that he was shaking. Shaking all over. He turned and looked at me and I thought he was going to say something. But he never got it out. He wiped his hand across his eyes. Then he turned and started to run. Hard. The way you run from a nightmare.

He was past the edge of the school grounds and

heading west, across Smith's pasture, when I finally unfroze. Then, Cassidy's words came echoing through my mind. "Eventually, he's going to need you. . . ." I figured that the time had come. I stood up. I caught one glimpse of the crowd of kids standing outside the school door, staring. Well, Red, I thought, I don't think you've made an inconspicuous getaway this time, either.

Then I was running, too. Trying to catch up to Lance. Running had always been the one thing where I had the edge on him so I didn't think it would be hard to catch him. What I was going to do then was another question. I'd think about that when I got there.

Half a mile later, I wasn't so sure I'd need to worry about that part. I hadn't gained on him at all and I was running out of wind. I ran on the school cross-country team and I was in pretty good shape but everyone knows you don't run distance at the pace Lance was setting. I guess everyone but Lance knew it. He still wasn't slowing down.

Then I realized that he was heading straight for the river. It was only about a mile away and, one thing for sure, it would stop him. Nobody swims the Whitewater at this time of year. If he was planning on getting across, he'd have to angle over to the highway bridge. I took a chance and cut the angle sharper. I was right. He turned the same direction.

I'd cut the distance between us to about a hundred yards by the time he reached the steep embankment that led up to the highway. Even then he barely slowed down. He ran right up it and disappeared from sight.

I made myself keep running. Soon, even over the sound of my own breathing, I could hear the river. The Whitewater is a mountain river. It starts fifty or sixty miles west of here, way up in the high country, and sometimes in the late spring when we get a lot of rainy weather mixed with some real hot days that river goes wild with run-off from the snow up there. Now was one of those times. As I came in sight of it I could see that it was full to the banks, coffee-coloured with mud, and sweeping along big rafts of driftwood and uprooted trees.

Gasping for breath, I scrambled up onto the highway grade and looked out along the high bridge. Lance was there. Right in the middle. Not running any more, just standing there, leaning on the railing and staring down into the foaming water. I was soaked with sweat from that run in the hot sun, but all at once I went cold. He wasn't thinking of . . . No, that wasn't Lance. But then I remembered the look in his eyes just before he started to run, and I wasn't so sure. I wasn't sure of anything right now. Except that I was scared. Scared to go up there, to do anything that would push him any more. Scared not to go . . .

"Be there." The words replayed in my mind one more time. Cassidy was usually right. I hoped to heaven that she was right this time. Slowly, I walked out onto the bridge.

"Hey, Lance," I tried to say as I came up behind him. But I was so out of breath that it came out as a hoarse little squeak that disappeared into the roar of the river. If Lance heard me, he didn't let on. From the way his shoulders were heaving, I guessed he was just as winded as I was.

I came up beside him and leaned on the railing. He didn't look up but I could sense that he knew I was there.

It seemed like we stood there for a long time. I guess a few cars went by but they seemed far away, in a different world. The only things that were real were Lance and me, and the roar of the river.

Finally I couldn't take the tension any longer, the not knowing how things stood between us. I had to try.

I reached over and put my hand on Lance's shoulder. I felt his muscles tense under my hand and I wondered if he was going to turn around and drive me one. I got a sudden vision of us fighting right there on the edge of the bridge, struggling above that raging water. It would have made a good movie scene.

But Lance didn't move. Didn't even look up. He wasn't going to make it easy for me. "Hey, man," I started, sounding stupid and feeling stupider, "Look, what I said back at the school I didn't mean to. I didn't mean to hit you." I swallowed hard. "Lance, I'm sorry." It was the best I could do. But I wasn't sure it would be good enough.

Lance raised his head and looked at me. His face was wet. I tried to read his eyes but I couldn't sort out everything I saw there. Disbelief? Anger? Pain? Mostly pain, I think. Slowly, he shook his head. "You're sorry?" he said in a soft, bitter voice. "You don't know what sorry means."

I didn't understand what he meant. That he didn't believe me? I couldn't think of anything else to say and I guess he couldn't either. He turned back to staring into the water. I did the same. The roar of the river was so loud that it made the rest of the world seem silent, gone.

After a long time Lance bent down and picked up a pebble. He dropped it over the side and we watched as the speed of the current carried it downstream a couple of feet before it sank out of sight. "I thought she was dead," he said, without looking up. His voice sounded empty, like there was nothing left inside him. "Oh, I knew she ran out on us all right. You can understand a lot at five. The night she left, I think even then I knew, deep down, that she was going." He looked up at me then and asked, "Remember that medal I always used to wear?"

Remember it? I could hardly forget it. It was still in my jacket pocket, right where I'd put it after I picked it up that rainy night. Just in time, I stopped my hand from reaching for it. One thing for sure, this was not the time to give it back. I just nodded and Lance went on.

"She gave it to me that night. If you can call it giving. I didn't even know I had it until after she was gone. I remember how she came into my room real late, after I'd been asleep for a long time. I was only about half-awake but something about the way she was acting scared me. She put her arms around me and held me and talked for a long while about how much she loved me." Lance's voice was still bitter but, just for a second, his eyes weren't, as he said, "I couldn't understand why she had to wake me up in the middle of the night just to tell me something I already knew." He turned away from me and looked down at the water again.

"Then I guess I went back to sleep, because I dreamed about a beautiful queen who gave me a medal on a golden chain. A magic charm, she said, to keep me from ever getting hurt . . .

"When I woke up the next morning, the medal was real. I was wearing it around my neck. But the queen was gone — and so was my mother.

"It was a St. Christopher's Medal. The patron saint of travellers. That had to be pretty funny. I wasn't going anywhere. It was her that was leaving. Anyway," and his voice got real soft so I could barely hear, "it isn't magic. It doesn't stop you from gettin' hurt."

I wanted to say something but sometimes there isn't anything to say. So I just stood there, scratching a loose flake of paint off the railing and waiting for Lance to start talking again. It seemed a long time later when he finally did.

"At first, I was so sure she was coming back. Every day, I'd ask Dad, 'Is she coming today?' I don't remember what he answered, but I know he never lied to me. And he never put her down, either. He'd just shake his head and say something like, 'Your mom needs some time to live her own life.'

"After a long time, I don't know, months, maybe years, I had to stop kidding myself. She wasn't coming back. So, then I convinced myself that it was because she couldn't come back. That she'd died in a car crash or got cancer or something. I used to lie awake at night when I was a little kid, thinking about it. About her dying there alone somewhere. And then I'd cry myself to sleep. But there was still something to hang onto. The beautiful queen who cared enough to come back . . ." He took a deep, ragged breath and added, "It sure beat the truth, anyway."

The river's roar filled the silence as Lance bent over and picked up another stone. As hard as he could, he heaved it out into the churning current. Then he turned to look at me. "Why couldn't she have just stayed dead?" he asked, like he really expected me to come up with an answer. "I could love her when she was dead," he added in a hoarse, almost-whisper, so low that I almost missed it. "Why'd she have to come back?"

He slammed his fist into the steel railing in front of him. He hit it again and again, like he was trying to hurt himself, to do something to bring all the pain outside where he could understand it.

I grabbed his wrist. "Quit it, Lance," I yelled, surprising myself with the authority in my voice. I think it surprised him too. He gave me a sideways look and I felt the tension slowly drain out of his muscles.

I let go then and he stood there for a minute, staring at his bleeding knuckles. Then he leaned his face against the railing and started to cry.

That was when I knew for sure that we were friends again. Lance was no hood, in spite of the way he had been acting, and there was nothing hard or mean about him. But he was tough and he'd learned a long time ago to hide his feelings and stay cool on the outside no matter what happened. And he was proud, so proud he'd die before he ever let on about just how tore up he really was. One thing was for sure. Lance Ducharme didn't cry in front of his enemies.

I stood there beside him, staring down into the water. There was nothing I could do or say to make things any easier but, somehow, I knew that Lance really wanted me to be there again. And I wanted to be there, too.

17

"Skippin' out, eh boys?" Neither of us heard the car pull up until the door slammed.

I jumped, my thoughts immediately turning to my dad. This would be one great time for him to show up. I turned around, half-expecting to see the cop car.

Instead I saw a white Corvette. Good old Randy himself. I wasn't particularly relieved to see him. If Dad had been the last person I wanted to see right then, Randy was running him a photo-finish second.

Then I took a good look at Randy and realized that he was completely wrecked. Like, right out of the picture. His eyes were lit up like the Las Vegas strip and he was so hyper he was practically bouncing. I didn't know what he'd been into this time but it had to be more than grass. Just being near him was making me nervous.

As I stood there looking at Randy I sensed, more than saw, Lance turn around to face him. "What'd you bring him along for?" Randy asked Lance, jerking his head in my direction.

Lance didn't say anything. He'd stopped crying but one look at him should have been enough to tell anybody he was still plenty shook. But Randy wasn't noticing the finer points. "Well, where's the money for the stuff?" he asked in a loud voice, as if more volume would get him more answers.

"Didn't get it," Lance muttered, staring at his worn running shoes.

Randy's face turned mean. "Hey, man, we had a deal . . ." But he broke off and I realized that he was staring over our heads, his attention focused on something beyond us. Slowly I turned to follow his gaze.

You can see all over town from that high bridge and it finally occurred to me what Randy had seen to freeze him like a bird dog spotting a pheasant.

It was a cop car, turning onto Main Street and heading west toward the bridge and toward us. It was still way over in the centre of town, nearly a mile away, and just cruising along at the speed limit, no siren, no lights. Probably they were going up to Jimmy the Greek's cafe for coffee, like they did about this time every afternoon.

But that wasn't how Randy had it figured. He freaked. Totally. He started yelling at me. Screaming like a maniac. Calling me names that would have made the bathroom poet blush. Hollering all this garbage about how we'd set him up, led him into a trap, and how that was my old man coming to pick him up in that cop car.

Even for Randy that was a new high in complete stupidity. I mean, that was an RCMP car down there, for cryin' out loud, not the town-cop car. My dad wasn't even there. He was probably down at the other end of town, getting his jollies ambushing speeders in the school zone.

I'd had about enough of Randy and I hoped he did get picked up, but right now I had other things on my mind. All I wanted between me and Randy was space — a lot of it. "Nothin's happening, Randy," I said tiredly, starting to push past him. "Just get off my case. I'm leavin'."

Suddenly, there was a click, and I found myself staring at six inches of shiny steel. A switchblade! I couldn't believe it. A switchblade in Alderton?

I had a wild desire to laugh, but he was holding that knife about two inches from my throat and, twitchy as he was, that didn't leave much margin for error. That thought sobered me up considerably.

"You ain't goin' nowhere," he snarled, and I stood very still.

Lance took a step forward, a look of total disbelief on his face. "Hey, Randy, come on, man. Cool it. Put that knife away. Red didn't do nothin'."

Randy's gaze shifted to Lance, but the knife didn't move. "Oh, no, he didn't do nothin'," Randy sneered. "Yesterday you're all hot to start dealin' for me. Then, all of a sudden, he shows up with you and everything's changed. You didn't get the money. I bet you didn't. You're just tryin' to make sure you come out clean when this little rat turns me in to his old man."

Lance shook his head. "You really have fried your brain this time, Borowski," he said, his voice edged with contempt. "There's no set up. No bust. Nothin'. If you don't believe me, just get in your car and split. Head for the border for all I care. But me and Red are gettin' out of here, now." Lance took another step — and Randy moved so fast I didn't even know what was happening. Now he was behind me with his arm around my neck and the knife pressed tight under my chin. I couldn't see the blade, but I could feel it. It felt cold. The same way my insides felt. A picture kept flashing through my mind. Something I'd seen at Silverwinds a couple of months ago when Lance and I had helped Mike butcher a steer for meat. After Mike had shot it, he cut its throat. One slash. About the same place Randy's knife was touching my throat now. One slash and a thousand pound steer had been bled dry in a matter of seconds . . . I took a deep breath and tried to keep my hands from shaking.

"Freeze, Injun!" Randy snarled at Lance. "Unless you want me to get you a pretty red scalp to hang on your belt." He laughed hysterically and I could feel the knife quiver against my throat.

Lance didn't take another step but his face went white and his eyes were smouldering. I don't know if it was because of the way Randy had sneered that word, "Injun," or because he'd pulled the knife on me, but in that second I think Lance would have killed him if he'd had the chance.

But he didn't have the chance. In this poker game Randy had all the aces. It was weird. Any other time, knife or no knife, Randy wouldn't have scared me. He came on as a tough guy but everybody knew that he was really a gutless wonder when he ran up against anything that couldn't be solved by either his money or his mouth. But right now there was no way I was ready to take the chance of crossing him. Because, whatever he was on, he was crazy. Totally irrational. And dangerous.

Keeping the knife pressed so tight I hardly dared to breathe, he nodded toward the car. "Start walk-in'," he said. He didn't sound much like Humphrey Bogart, either, but I felt like I'd landed in the middle of an old gangster movie. Then he looked at Lance. "You too, Injun. Go first." Lance didn't move. I could see his eyes measuring the chances. For a second I thought he was going to go for Randy, but then the tension seemed to ease out of him and the tiger-look was gone from his eyes. I knew he'd read the situation the same way I had. Lance was fast but no move he could make would be fast enough to beat that knife. He gave Randy a look that should have left third-degree burns but he walked over to the car.

Randy made Lance get in first. Then he dragged

me around to the driver's side and pushed me in. He made me crawl across the console and into the other bucket seat with Lance. And only a few weeks ago I had willingly sardined myself into that same seat, just to get out of the rain . . .

Thinking back on it, now, maybe we missed our best chance to jump Randy right then, when he was starting the car and pulling back onto the road. But it didn't look so easy at the time. For one thing, we were still stunned by the whole business and I think we kept expecting that it was some crazy joke that would soon be over. That, and the fact that while Randy's left hand turned the key, his right kept the knife real close to my throat. Too close to do anything stupid.

Then the motor caught and Randy tramped on the gas. I stared with awe as that car accelerated so fast that the force threw us back against the seat like astronauts at blast-off. It reminded me of a story Greg had told me once about one of his friends. This kid used to have a pretty cool money-making scheme. He'd take a ten-dollar bill and put it on the dash and then bet whoever was riding in the passenger seat that they couldn't lean forward and grab that bill in a certain number of seconds. If they couldn't, they owed the driver a ten. According to Greg, that car was so hot that his friend never lost. I didn't believe that story when he told it to me, but I did now. If Randy ever went out of drug-dealing, I knew how he could pick up the odd ten.

The only thing that distracted me from watching the speedometer was the knife. Every time Randy reached down to shift the steel flashed in the sun. It looked like a good knife. Sharp.

Now the speedometer needle was vibrating steadily between 90 and 100 mph. Randy drove one-handed and spent half his time gawking at us instead of watching the road. That, combined with the fact that he was so stoned he would have been dangerous driving a wheelbarrow, helped me make up my mind about one thing. There was no way I was going to do anything to mess up what was left of his concentration. Maybe he'd end up knifing us both, but I figured that the chances of that happening didn't even come close to the chances of us getting splattered all over some power pole if he lost control now.

Whatever happened, it would happen later. Right now, it was waiting time.

I sat still, scrunched into a position that was fast putting my right leg to sleep, watching the scenery blur past, and wondering where Randy was taking us for this free vacation. We were heading south. Mexico, maybe. Sometimes, when school hit an all-time record for terminal boredom, I'd dream about just driving away, heading for Mexico. But I don't think this was quite what I'd had in mind . . .

Randy hit the radio switch and the loud rock beat filled the car. Randy jerked his right hand to the beat. Flash, flash went the knife. Up and down. Up and down. Close. Too close. "Another One Bites the Dust." That was the name of the song. Come on, Randy, watch what you're doing! I didn't want it to be my epitaph, too.

18

We stayed on the highway for quite a ways. There wasn't much traffic which was a good thing the way Randy was driving. He passed everything he caught up with and, at the speed he was going, he caught up with most everything that was going the same way we were. And he passed them where he found them. Hills, curves, nothing bothered him. Everything bothered me but, fortunately, I was too scared to even open my mouth.

Suddenly he hit the brakes, slowed down to a speed suitable for a curve on the Indianapolis Speedway, and, taking the corner on two wheels, swung onto a sideroad and headed west. And I'd thought I'd been scared on the highway . . .

There was a lot of loose gravel on the sideroad and, while the Corvette handled like its wheels were glued to pavement, this was a different story. It was like the wheels had suddenly retracted and we were whipping back and forth across the surface of the road like a speedboat skimming across a lake.

Now my stomach is a legend in its own time (unless it gets punched right after lunch). I'm the kind of person who can eat three helpings of lasagna at home, go to the rodeo and stuff myself with every kind of garbage food on the midway, last through five consecutive rides on the tilt-a-whirl, and come out ready for a pizza. But a few more of these curves and I knew I was going to barf. I glanced at Lance. I would never have believed he could look that pale. I closed my eyes. When we finally went into orbit, I didn't want to witness the blast-off. The radio was playing "Jump" by Van Halen. I wished I could.

When I'd about decided that this ride would last for the rest of my life, however brief that might be, Randy hit the brakes again. We skidded sideways into a driveway and screeched to a stop in front of a log cabin that almost blended into the pine forest that surrounded it.

Randy grabbed me by the collar and, holding the knife close enough to keep my attention, in a slurred voice he ordered, "Out. This side." I was so stiff I could hardly move but I managed to scramble across the console and almost fall out of the car on the driver's side. Still holding onto me, Randy nodded to Lance. "Okay, Injun, now you." Lance got out and walked around the car.

"Over to the cabin," Randy commanded. We walked. On the porch, he jerked me to a stop. "Key's on the ledge above the door. You get it," he said to Lance. Lance got it. He turned it in the lock and the door creaked open.

"Get inside," Randy snarled. Slowly Lance stepped through the door. We followed, with Randy still dragging me around by the collar like a disobedient puppy.

The stale, musty smell of long emptiness swept out to meet us. I remembered hearing that Randy's dad had a summer cabin somewhere west of Calgary. This must be it, I supposed. The place was old and dusty and neglected-looking — not the kind of summer cabin they show in *Better Homes and Gar-*

dens. But I could see that it still must be used once in a while. There was quite a bit of furniture in it. A big wooden table with chairs around it, a couch and a couple of worn leather armchairs, and a huge, old black woodstove that practically filled one end of the room. A closed door led to another room.

I checked the front window. Pretty high and small. Not the sort of window you should try to jump through. I turned my head to see the north window and Randy's hand tightened on my collar. His fingers dug into me like claws as he jerked me back so hard my head spun. That hurt! Now my temper took over and all my fear drowned in a sea of red fury. "Get your hands off me!" I yelled and, without stopping to think, I turned my head and sunk my teeth into the hand on my collar. It could have been the last bite I ever took. I'll never know why I didn't get stabbed right then. Maybe, for a second, Randy was too stunned even to remember that he had the knife. It seemed that way because instantly, the hand that had been holding my shirt let go and, in the same movement, smashed me a good one across the mouth.

Red stars flashed through a black sky and I staggered backward, thinking vaguely that this was the second time I'd got slugged today and that I'd had about enough of it. Then the wall slammed into my back, bringing me to a sudden stop and keeping me from falling down. Randy started toward me. "You little . . ." he began, in a voice like broken glass, but I never had the pleasure of hearing yet another of his affectionate descriptions of me.

"Quit it, Randy!" Lance's voice crackled through the air, as menacing as electric current sparking from a broken wire. He took a step forward but, quick as a cat, Randy swung around to meet him, grabbing his shirt and flinging him back onto the couch behind him.

"You stay outa this!" Randy screeched. "Just stay there and keep your mouth shut!" Then he turned on me again. "It's all your fault!" he said. "You set me up. They're out there now. Waitin' to come and get me!" He pulled back the curtain and stared, wild-eyed, out into the emptiness of the silent pine forest. "They're sneakin' up out there. Cops! Hundreds of them. They think they're gonna bust in here and get me. But when they do . . ." he started to laugh, a high-pitched, crazy laugh, " . . .when they do, your old man's gonna be disappointed. 'Cause you're gonna be dead!"

He took another step toward me. And another. There was nowhere for me to run. The wall was behind me. He was in front. I stood there, staring at him. I'd heard about snakes hypnotizing their prey with their eyes but this was the first time I had really understood it. I couldn't look away from Randy's wild, glittering eyes. All at once I remembered something I had seen a long time ago. The setting sun reflecting off the west windows of an old, abandoned house. Randy's eyes were just like those windows — all lit up but with only emptiness inside them.

That was when it registered on me just how far out of control Randy really was. He's going to kill me. This guy is so burnt that he's actually going to take that knife and kill me . . . I was so scared that my mind went kind of numb, almost like I'd gone right through scared and come out the other side of it. It felt like I was a reporter, standing back on top of a hill somewhere, and taking notes on everything that was going on in that room. Randy was still screaming at me but I had tuned out the words, tuned him right out just like a bad song on the radio . . .

Then, in spite of being frozen solid inside, something got through to me enough to make me look across the room at Lance. He was still on the couch where Randy had pushed him, but the way he was sitting there reminded me of something. Suddenly I knew what it was. A cat. A cat sitting in the grass, absolutely motionless but coiled like a spring, ready to leap at the first hint of a mouse-rustle. For a split-second, his eyes met mine, and I knew . . . Don't try it, Lance! The thought flashed through my mind but I didn't have time to even start to say it because he went for the knife. With one jump, he landed on Randy from behind and the two of them hit the floor.

For a second, everything was a tangle of thrashing bodies and I couldn't tell who had who down. My first instinct was to jump into it, too, but it looked like Lance was on top so I held back. Then they rolled again and Randy seemed to be taking control. Lance was a big, strong kid for his age and a good fighter, but Randy had four years and thirty pounds on him. Even with Randy so zonked he could hardly see, Lance didn't really have a chance. I had to do something to even the odds.

My eyes swept the room and came to rest on a pile of split wood by the stove. I grabbed a stick and swung it at Randy's scraggly blond hair. There was a dull thud and Randy groaned and collapsed.

A terrible thought hit me. I dropped to my knees and rolled him over on his back. When I saw that he was breathing I started breathing again, too. I'd been scared when I thought he was going to kill me, but I'd been just as scared when I thought I might have killed him.

Now a wild surge of relief flowed through me. I jumped to my feet. "Hey, all right!" I yelled, turning back toward Lance. "We did . . ." I began, but then I saw Lance and the rest of the sentence died. He was standing up but there was something about him . . . It was his eyes that I noticed first. They looked huge. And shocked. The way a deer's eyes look when they get caught in the headlights at night. Then I saw the reason for that look and my stomach turned into a lump of ice.

The knife. Lance had grabbed it all right. But it was the blade that he'd grabbed. He was still holding it clenched in his fist as he stood there, holding his wrist with the other hand and staring unbelievingly at the little red rivers that trickled between his fingers and dropped in bright spatters onto the bare wood floor. Then, real slow, as if remembering which muscles to move took a lot of concentration, he opened his hand. The knife hit the floor with a bang that sounded startlingly loud in the sudden silence. The red rivers flowed faster. The spatters on the floor grew into a pool.

I couldn't stop staring. Way back in my mind a voice was saying, "Hey, man, you better do something . . ." but the rest of me was too numb to react. Vaguely I wondered how long it took a person to bleed to death, and all those old St. John's Ambulance First Aid films we'd had in health class came flashing back through my mind, in Technicolor!

They had been great. There was always some kid who just couldn't handle the sight of all that red dye spurting out all over the place and either tossed his cookies or passed out cold on the floor. But not me! The gorier the better. I'd passed that first aid test so many times I should have been licensed to do heart transplants. But now I was finding out that real life was a whole lot different than "Fun With First Aid." This time the blood was real. And it was my best friend that was doing the bleeding.

I might have stood there in a daze until he really did bleed to death if Lance hadn't brought me back to reality. He took a deep, shaky breath and then said, dead serious, "Well, Paleface, what you waitin' for? Now's your big chance. All you have to do is cut yourself a little, too, and we can be blood brothers, just like in those old movies." He flashed that famous grin of his. It didn't show up quite as white as usual because his face was kind of white, too, but the dazed look was gone from his eyes. Lance was okay. He might be cut up pretty bad but he was still in better shape than I'd seen him for a long time.

I started grinning, too, and then we were both laughing, I guess that's when I started to come unfrozen and realize that I'd better do something, fast. I tore open drawers until I found one with some dish towels in it. I grabbed a handful.

Lance had sunk down into a chair and laid his right hand on the table, still holding tight to the wrist with his other hand. There was blood all over the place and I could barely see where the cut was. I wasn't so sure I wanted to see it, anyway. I rolled one towel up into a little ball and pressed it into the palm of his hand and started winding another towel around as tight as I could to keep it in place. It didn't look as neat as my First Aid Course bandages did. Nobody ever bled all over them.

Lance looked at the bandage and then grinned up at me. "Hey," he said, "you're supposed to reassure the patient. The way you're shakin' isn't reassurin' me much."

"Well, if you'd quit bleeding this would work a lot better," I muttered, worriedly, trying to get the bandage tighter.

"Hey, man, I ain't doin' it on purpose," he said, laughing at me.

"Try closing your hand. That might help."

He shook his head. "I can't."

A cold chill swept through me and I looked up to meet his eyes. "You mean it hurts too much to close it?" I asked hopefully.

"No," he said, his voice calm. "It's still too numb to hurt much at all. I mean when I try to close it nothin' happens."

I couldn't think of anything to say in answer to that. All the thoughts that came to mind were too scary to put into words.

"I guess I'm gonna have to get stitches in it, huh?" he said, sounding disgusted.

Yeah, about five hundred, I thought, feeling sick. I shrugged. "Yeah, maybe a few," I said. My voice was unconcerned but my mind was racing in panicked circles.

There wasn't a phone in the cabin. All the places anywhere near were weekend cabins so the odds were against finding anyone home on a Wednesday afternoon. Whatever happened next, it looked like it was going to be up to me to make it happen. But while I was still figuring that out, Lance stood up. "Come on," he said. "Your thrill of a lifetime is about to happen."

"Huh?" I said blankly.

Lance grinned. "The hottest car in Alderton is waitin' outside. I don't think Randy wants to drive and I'd sure flip you for the chance but my daddy always makes me keep both hands on the wheel. So, I guess that leaves you."

"The Corvette!" I said, awe-struck.

"Yeah, I know it ain't much but it'll beat walkin'."

I came to life. "All right! Let's give her a shot!" Then I caught a glimpse of Randy just starting to move and groan a little. "Hang on," I told Lance. "Gotta tidy up before we go."

The cabin had one of those old-fashioned trap-door cellars, just a big, dirt-floored hole under the floor to keep vegetables and stuff. And since old Randy seemed to be doing his best to make himself into a vegetable, I figured it would be a good place to keep him for a while. At least down there he couldn't do much harm to himself or anyone else.

I yanked the trap door open. Randy didn't resist

as I dragged his big, limp body across the floor and let his legs dangle into the hole. It was only another couple of feet to the bottom so I just kind of gently dropped him in. Then I shut the trap door and pulled the heavy old, oak table over on top of it. That should hold him for a while.

I walked over to where Lance was leaning against the doorframe. "Okay," I said. "Let's go see if Randy's old car's got anything under the hood."

What I didn't tell him was that I'd never driven anything with a standard transmission before. I had a feeling that he'd find out soon enough.

19

I opened the door and helped Lance in on the passenger side. Then I got behind the wheel. "Okay, hang on," I said, reaching out to turn the key. Key? What key? There was no key in the ignition.

"Red," Lance said patiently. "I'm hangin' on. What are we waitin' for?"

"Well, you're gonna have to keep hangin'. The key's not here."

"Of course it ain't. Randy put it in his pocket when he got out of the car."

I couldn't believe this was happening. "Great! Just great!" I muttered as I jumped out of the car. I tore back into the cabin, moved the table, and, hoping that Randy hadn't perked up too much, flung open the trap door. Randy was still in a heap. I checked his jacket pockets. Nothing but a pack of cigarettes. Must be in his jeans. I rolled him over. "Mmmph," he said, which was about as intelligent as his usual conversations.

I found the key. I dumped Randy back in his heap, scrambled up the ladder, went through all the steps again in reverse order, and landed in the car out of breath. Lance gave me a stony look. "Red, ol' buddy," he said.

"What?" I muttered, fitting the key into the ignition.

"Next time I need an emergency trip to the hospital, don't drive me, okay? I'll just walk and save time."

That didn't deserve an answer. I stepped on the clutch, just in case I hadn't managed to get the car out of gear, fed it some gas and turned the key. That big old engine came to life with a satisfying growl. I wiggled the shift lever around. "That's gotta be first gear," I announced as I leaned on the gas pedal and popped the clutch.

The car shot ahead like a racehorse coming out of the starting gate. Then it stalled.

"I don't think that was first," Lance observed.

I ignored him and tried again. A different gear and a little less gas. The car lurched, bucked a couple of times and took off across the yard. I was so surprised I almost drove into a tree, but I did some fancy steering and got it pointed toward the road. I picked the opposite direction from the way we had come. There had to be a faster way to civilization than that scenic tour Randy had brought us on.

I gave it a little more gas. The motor roared like an irritated lion but the car didn't speed up much. Lance gave me a weary look. "Hate to tell you this, Red, but you can't just keep goin' in first gear. You gotta shift."

"I know, I know. I'm workin' on it," I said, studying the shift lever with one eye and trying to keep the other on the road. There were a lot of curves and, after catching a glimpse of the drop-off to the river below, I figured it was best not to miss one.

I stepped on the clutch and tried for second. It slipped in, smooth as butter! "There she is!" I yelled triumphantly as I let out the clutch and fed her some gas. The engine screamed and the car coasted gently to a stop.

"Think you just discovered neutral," Lance said
helpfully.

"Ducharme, if you open that big mouth one more
time . . ." I found first gear on the first try this time
and started all over again. Finally, on a straight
stretch, I tried for second one more time. I made it. I
came pretty close to putting us in the opposite ditch,
but I made it.

"Red," said Lance, when he had quit holding his
breath, "Do me a favour. Don't try for third."

I laughed. I was starting to relax a little. Driving
the 'vette was great — once you got in gear. It was
one of those perfect, early-summer days, especially
out here in the hills, away from all the people and
traffic. I started day-dreaming . . .

We were a couple of spoiled-rotten rich brats, just
out cruisin' chicks in the car my filthy-rich parents
had given me for my eighteenth birthday (might as
well dream big). After a while, we'd go home, have a
swim in the indoor pool, and then give the polo ponies
a work-out . . .

Pretty stupid dream, huh? Well, it sure beat the
one about taking off from school, getting kidnapped
by a freaked-out, two-bit drug pusher, Lance getting
carved up with a switchblade, and me ending up
behind the wheel of a stolen car I couldn't handle
and heading for I wasn't sure where. That one wasn't
even a dream. It was a nightmare.

We came around another curve and a sign pointed
to an intersection ahead. I realized where we were —
coming out on the old Banff highway just a few miles
west of Cochrane. It wouldn't take long to get to
town.

I had a good view of the highway. No traffic in
sight. It was a good thing because no way was I
planning to stop that car again. I peeled out onto the
highway and headed east. "Hey," I said, "I finally

figured out . . ." I looked over at Lance to see if he was listening — and forgot what I had started to say. The bandage was soaked through and blood was slowly dripping onto the seat beside him. "Hey, man," I said, trying to sound cool and unconcerned. "You're bleedin' all over Randy's nice white seats."

Lance looked down at his hand. "Yeah," he said slowly, "and you don't know how bad I feel about messin' them up." He was grinning wickedly but this time his smile and his face were almost the same shade of white. I speeded up. When I hit 70 that engine was screaming like an elephant with a toothache. Almost without thinking, I reached for the shift. It went into third smoother than spaghetti sliding off your fork. Wow, was I good!

I hit the Cochrane town limits doing 85 and automatically started braking so I didn't pick up a cop. Then the reality of the situation hit me and I almost burst out laughing. Man, would I love to pick up a cop right now! The most beautiful sight in the world would be a big, old police car in my rear view mirror, siren howling and party lights flashing. I wouldn't care what he did to me — he could even take away my licence (which I wouldn't have for another ten months), just as long as he took control of this whole mess.

But, naturally, there wasn't a cop in sight. Cochrane must have more cops than any other small town in the world — I've never gone through there without seeing at least two cars. Until today, that is.

"They got a hospital in this town?" Lance asked.

I shook my head. "Don't think so. People around here are supposed to go to Calgary to be sick. But there's gotta at least be a doctor's office . . ." I moved into the right lane, ready to turn off into the business district.

"Don't, Red."

"Huh?"

"Don't stop here."

"What?" I turned to stare at him and almost drove into a Toyota in the other lane. "What are you talkin' about?" I said as I steered back to where I belonged and tried to ignore the sign language from the Toyota's driver.

Lance's voice sounded tired. "Come on, Red. If we do find a doctor here he probably won't just fix this in his office. He'll send me to Calgary anyhow. And I don't feel much like bein' passed around like a biology specimen all day. Anyhow," he added, "I'm not sure I've got that much time to waste wandering around here."

Lance was *asking* to go to the hospital? He hated hospitals.

For the first time since he'd grabbed that knife, he was sounding a little bit scared. And Lance didn't scare easy . . . I glanced over at him again, this time remembering to keep one eye on the road. There was a lot of blood now, and he was leaning back against the seat with his eyes closed. From the way he was sweating, I figured that the numbness had about worn off.

"Hurtin' pretty bad?" I asked.

"It don't exactly tickle," he said slowly. Coming from Lance, that meant it hurt bad enough.

I sighed. "You think I'm gonna drive this thing into the city. That what you've got in mind?"

Lance managed a grin. "You got it, Paleface."

"Geronimo, you are one glutton for punishment."

He opened his eyes and turned to look at me. "You gonna do it?"

"Yeah."

We hit the city limits at a quarter to five. Timed it perfect to the minute. Rush hour — dead centre. The only good thing about it was that traffic was so tied up that things moved slow enough for me to figure out what I was doing as I went along. But the bad part was that we seemed to hit every red light in the whole city. And that meant starting and stopping a few dozen times. People aren't exactly polite when you kill the engine in the middle of an intersection. I ought to know — that's what I did three times in the first five sets of lights.

I kept my eye open for a cop. Anybody driving the way I was should have attracted cops like picnics attract ants. I expected a flashing light to appear in my mirror any second. I kept hoping it would. But on the whole trip I only saw one cop car. And it was going in the opposite direction. The cop didn't even look my way. Even my red hair seemed to have failed me as an attention-getter. So all I could do was keep driving, straight ahead.

I knew there was a hospital in the west part of the city but I've never been there and I wasn't about to take a chance of getting the wrong turn-off. Eastside Hospital was away across the city but it was the only hospital I'd been to so I decided to play it safe — well, I guess safe wasn't really the word I would have chosen to describe anything connected with this trip. But at least it would help to have some faint clue where I was going.

I wished we could get moving. These two and three light waits were driving me crazy. And the silence was getting to me. As long as Lance had been talking to me, I figured he wasn't in too bad a shape. But he'd been quiet all the way from Cochrane, just sitting there with his eyes closed — bleeding. I tried to think of something to say but this didn't seem like the time to discuss how the Expos were doing and any subject that seemed important right now was too depressing to start on.

It was Lance who finally broke the silence. "Hey, Red, I'm sorry I got you mixed up in all this," he

said right out of the blue, just as if I'd been com-
plaining about it or something. His voice sounded
real tired and, when I glanced over at him, he looked
just plain miserable. For a while, back there, he'd
been his old self, arrogant and laughing, in control
of the situation. But he sure didn't look that way
now. Maybe it was the pain and all the blood he'd
lost. That could have been part of it but I didn't
think that was what was really getting to him. I figured he'd had enough time to start thinking too much
again.

"Come on," I said. "It was Randy that kidnapped
me, not you. And when you took off from school, I
followed you. Remember? As far as I could see, you
were doin' your best to get away from me — which
you couldn't, you bein' such a lousy runner . . ." I
threw him a challenging grin, trying to make him
lighten up and fight back.

He didn't grin back when he answered. "That's
'cause I wanted you to catch up." And I was left
wondering if he was throwing the challenge back to
me or giving me one heck of a big compliment.

The light changed and traffic started crawling
again. I was still three cars back when I saw the light
flash orange again. The two cars ahead of me speeded up a little to make it through and I floored it. That
Corvette was some car! Still not a cop in sight.

I wondered if I dared bring up the subject that
was on my mind. It would be one sure way to keep
Lance's attention. "You're takin' all this stuff with
your mother too serious," I said, hoping I wasn't
starting something that was going to end up in another fight. But he didn't say anything so I went on.
"Look, I don't blame you for being mad at her for
coming back that way. I don't think I could handle
something like that, either. But it's you you're tearin'
up about it, not her. Why don't you just sit down

with her, be polite, and say, 'So, what you been doin' for the last ten years, Mom?' Let her get all her stored-up guilt out of her system and then she'll get out of your life for another ten years.''

"She's not gonna get out of my life," Lance said, his voice low and tense.

Something in the way he said it made me nervous. "What do you mean?" I asked.

There was a long silence. "She wants custody," he said at last, and I turned to stare at him, wondering if I'd heard right. Another light went red and I almost put us through the windshield, braking to keep from hitting the car in front of us.

Custody. The word bounced off the sides of my mind. I knew what it meant, all right, but I couldn't apply it to Lance. Custody battles were like in *Kramer vs. Kramer.* Parents fighting over who was going to raise some little six-year-old kid. Not over Lance who was already more grown up than a lot of adults would ever be. But then I realized that I was seeing it from my point of view, not the law's. Lance wasn't even sixteen yet. He was too young. But he was too old. Way too old. Maybe five years ago it wouldn't have been too late for Anne-Marie. Or maybe it was like he had told her there at The Cliffs. Maybe it had always been too late — ever since the day she had walked away from him.

"Yeah," Lance added. "She came out to the ranch and laid it on the line. That's what she wants and she's going to fight for it, in court. Tomorrow. Tonight's her big concert and tomorrow's her big performance for the judge."

"Custody?" I said it out loud as we sat idling at a light. "Hey, man, that doesn't even make sense. She can't just wander off for ten years and then suddenly reappear and expect a judge to congratulate her on being such a great mother and hand you over to her just like that. Don't sweat it, Lance. She hasn't got a chance in court."

Lance interrupted me. "Red, you're talkin' about how it should be. I'm talkin' about how it is. You know my dad, and now you know my . . ." he hesitated, "you know, her. Who's gonna talk the best show when it comes to court? Can you see my dad with some big-time lawyer tearin' him apart?"

Yeah, I could see that all right. And it didn't make a very nice picture. "Okay," I said. "So it's gonna be a bad scene. But she's still gonna lose. She hasn't really got anything goin' for her. You can't win a court case on charm . . ."

"She's got more than charm," Lance interrupted, his voice hoarse. "Remember that time Dad caught me smokin' in the barn . . ." He didn't finish that sentence. He didn't have to. That was one incident I wasn't likely to ever forget. "Well, somehow she found out about that. And," Lance swallowed hard, "she says she's got witnesses that will swear that Dad isn't a fit parent."

I sat there, trying to think of something to say. The blast of a horn saved me. I let out the clutch too fast and we bucked our way through the intersection.

"But," Lance went on, "those people don't know nothin' about what it takes to be a good father. They weren't there when I was eight years old and so sick with scarlet fever I was delirious. I can still remember it like it happened yesterday. I was seein' snakes. Big green ones with red eyes. They were all over the place, comin' at me. And I was so scared. And then, like magic, Dad was there, sittin' on the bed beside me. I told him about those snakes and he put his arm around me and he said, 'Don't you let those snakes worry you none. Before they can get to you, they got to get past me, and I ain't gonna let them . . .' And, right then, I stopped bein' scared.

"And then there was that morning, back in grade six, when Tomte came limping up to the house with his leg all mangled. Dad dropped everything he was doing and took him to the vet. You know what he paid for gettin' that cat's leg amputated? A hundred bucks. You know how much work my dad has to do to earn a hundred bucks? He didn't have a hundred bucks just lyin' around. But he found it. For a mangy old cat. Because it was my mangy old cat . . .

"And even the lickings. The lickings that are supposed to make him some sort of a monster. I've never yet got anything I didn't deserve. And if he does get a little too rough sometimes, it's only because he cares too much and he's tryin' too hard. Tryin' to keep me from doin' anything to mess up my chances at having a better life than he's had. Tryin' to be two parents at once . . ." His voice broke and he was quiet a minute. Then he added, "Oh, yeah, he's a real lousy father, all right." I heard him swallow hard and take a deep breath but he couldn't stop his voice from shaking a little. "But none of the good stuff is gonna come out in court. What they're gonna hear is that Mike Ducharme is an ignorant, violent half-breed who beats his kid up bad enough to leave scars. That's what everybody's gonna remember . . ."

Lance was sitting up straight now and his eyes were almost burning holes in me. "I'm not gonna let her do that to him, Red. I can't let her."

I sighed, feeling like the whole world had just turned into one big, black, slippery-sided hole — with a bottom full of alligators. "You can't stop her, Lance," I said tiredly.

"Yeah, I can stop her," Lance said, and his voice sounded like he was in control again.

"How?" I asked, half-scared to hear his answer.

"If she gets what she wants, she won't need to take it to court."

"What do you mean?" I asked—but I didn't really want to know.

"I'm going with her."

The whole world was out of control. Things were happening too fast for me to handle them. All I knew for sure was that everything was all wrong. "No!" I burst out. "You can't do that! You shouldn't have to do it. It's not fair."

When Lance answered me his voice was soft, soft and bitter. "Life isn't fair, Red. Did it take you fifteen years to figure that out?"

When I looked over at him he was leaning against the door. His eyes were closed and his face was set with pain that was only partly physical.

I almost ran a red light. My mind was whirling so fast I was dizzy and my eyes were stinging so I had to blink hard to see the light at all.

20

I pulled into that Emergency Entrance, hit the brakes, forgot the clutch, and killed the engine. We jerked to a stop. Not a very classy finale to the ride of a life-time. But we'd made it. That was all that mattered. Suddenly I felt drained, totally. I breathed a sigh of relief and leaned my head against the steering wheel for a second. But only for a second. Lance's voice jerked me back. "Hey, Red, that's cheatin'. Anybody gets to pass out around here, it's gonna be me."

I looked over at him. He could still manage a weak grin but, from the way he looked and the faraway sound of his voice, I wondered how much of that comment was joke and how much was truth.

I opened the car door. "I'm going to get a doctor or something. Just take it easy. I'll be right back." I started to get out but his good hand shot out and grabbed my jacket.

"Forget it, Red. I may be damaged but I ain't dead. I made it this far. I'm walkin' in there with you."

It wasn't the time to start an argument. I went around and opened the door for him. Slowly he got out. He was a mess. The car seat was a mess. I didn't know anybody could bleed that much and still have any blood left inside them. He staggered a little as he stood up and I put my arm around him to steady him. Then I was a mess, too. I didn't think I'd ever enjoy another first-aid film.

A security guard met us at the door and, for some reason, I was sure he wasn't going to let us in, looking like we did and all. But I forgot this was an emergency room, not a school dance. He took one look at us and flung the door open wide. "Straight ahead," he said. "The nurse at the desk will help you."

Obviously that nurse had seen a little blood before. She never batted an eye. Just said, "This way, please," and headed off down a hall. We followed.

"Red?" Lance said, just above a whisper.

"Yeah?"

"Stick with me, okay?" His eyes met mine and said what the words hadn't. He really was scared. Then I remembered that hospitals weren't exactly his favourite places. I couldn't blame him. I was pretty nervous, too, and I didn't have a mark on me. "You got it, Geronimo. Just like blood brothers," I promised as the nurse led us into a little room.

Two minutes later, I found out that I wasn't going to get to keep that promise. The nurse helped me lay Lance down on a white-covered table and, suddenly, that room started filling up with white-covered people. Three or four of them were rushing in and out, rolling in trays of equipment, issuing orders to each other. Snatches of their conversation ran through my mind in unrelated chunks. ". . . pretty shocky . . . check pressure . . . get an IV started . . . see if Dr. McKelvey's available . . ."

Nobody seemed to notice I was there at first. They just stepped around me like I was a piece of furniture someone had left underfoot. Then, one of them asked, "How did this happen?" I didn't know who she was talking to but there were only two of us who knew the answer and I didn't think Lance felt like talking.

"Switchblade," I said, and a big nurse turned and

gave me a sharp look. I think that was the first time she had realized I was there.

"Wait outside, please," she said briskly, nodding toward the door.

"But . . ."

She took me firmly by the shoulder and pointed me toward the door. "Outside, please," she said in a tone that didn't make me feel like talking back. I gave Lance a helpless look as she practically pushed me out of the way. He closed his eyes.

Going out the door, I almost collided with a tall, skinny guy in a white coat. He didn't look much older than me but the tag on his coat read "Dr. Melvin" so I guessed he was older. Probably an intern, I decided from my vast knowledge of hospitals. (Well, sometimes if it's raining and there's nothing else to do I watch *General Hospital*.)

I guess I must have looked about as worried as I felt because, even though he seemed to be in a terrific hurry, he stopped and smiled. "Hey, relax, kid. He's not going to die on you. Things are just kind of hectic till we get him stabilized. You'll be able to see him in a little while. Why don't you go wash up and get yourself a Coke or something?" He disappeared into the room and the door closed behind him. He was the first human being I had met in this place. Come to think of it, he had red hair.

I looked at my hands and decided he was right about washing. I went hunting for a bathroom.

I almost scared myself when I looked in the mirror. It was hard to believe that I could have that much blood on me and none of it was mine. I washed my hands and face and that improved things a lot but I couldn't do much about my clothes. When I walked back into the waiting room they still looked like they'd just come off a battlefield.

The nurse at the desk spotted me as I walked by

and called me over. "You came in with the boy with the cut hand?"

I nodded. "Yeah."

"You're a friend of his?"

I nodded again.

"Okay, maybe I can get some information from you while they're working on him." She looked bored as she pulled out a form and started filling it out. I didn't see how anybody could be bored in an emergency room, but I guess you can get used to anything.

I gave her all the basic stuff. Name, address, age . . . When she got to parents, I told her Mike's name. "There's just his dad," I said and, as soon as I had said it, I realized that wasn't entirely true any more. But it was true enough not to complicate things. I let it go at that.

"Do you know his father's phone number?"

"Yeah. Do you want me to call him?"

"No, that's fine. We'll take care of it." I told her the number and she wrote it down. Then she skimmed on down the page until she found another question she thought I could answer. "Now," she said briskly. "How did this accident happen?" Obviously she was expecting an answer that would fit into the two-line blank. But I knew that even the condensed version would take a lot more than that . . .

"Well," I said slowly, "it wasn't exactly an accident . . ." I skipped all the parts about how we happened to meet up with Randy in the first place and just gave her the general story about him being so hyped up that he didn't know what he was doing, and how Lance had jumped him because he was waving that knife around like a maniac, threatening to kill me. She didn't ask how we got to the hospital so I didn't volunteer that part. But I couldn't get around the bit about knocking Randy out and locking him in the cellar. By the time I'd finished telling her about that she wasn't looking bored any more. She nodded, grabbed another kind of form, and scribbled a few words on it. Then, she looked at me. "How about you? Have you got a way home or shall I phone your parents?"

My stomach lurched. All afternoon, it had seemed like I'd been riding on an out-of-control roller coaster, with things happening so fast there hadn't even been time to think. Now, for the first time, I had time to wonder how Dad was going to react to everything that had happened. And I decided that I had liked the out-of-control roller coaster better . . .

"No, don't do that," I blurted out, and then quickly added, "You've got a lot of important stuff to do. I'll call them myself." Dad was going to have to hear this story; there was no getting away from it. And I figured he'd better hear it first-hand, from me.

"Okay," the nurse said. "I think that's all for now. Thanks. Oh, by the way, what's your name?"

I really didn't think she needed to know that but I didn't argue. I told her and she wrote it down. I was just going to ask her when I was going to get to see Lance when she turned away and picked up a phone. She dialled and listened for a couple of seconds. "Yes, Sergeant Bernelli. This is Eastside General . . ."

I thought she was supposed to be calling Lance's dad. Well, one thing was for sure, whoever she was talking to, she wasn't about to have time for me for a while. I wandered into the waiting room and sat down.

I tried to read a six-month-old *Life* magazine but that was no good. I couldn't concentrate. Then I tried watching the people coming and going around me. Normally that would have kept me interested for a long time. There were probably some pretty good stories behind the people who ended up in emergency rooms. But I couldn't concentrate on that either. The story behind what *I* was doing here had me too worried.

It seemed like a long time since they had taken Lance in there and, with all the blood he'd lost . . . What if . . . ? No, he was okay. Dr. Melvin had said he was okay. But then again, what did he know? Why should I believe a gawky, red-headed intern who looked like he should still be playing high-school basketball? I got up and started to pace.

I paced past the pay phone twice before the thought hit me. I had said that I would call Dad. And, if I didn't, I knew that eventually someone else would. There was no use in stalling any longer. I stuck my hand in my pocket, half-hoping I didn't have any change. But I did.

Slowly I fed the coins into the phone and dialled. It rang once. Twice. Maybe he wasn't home. And if he wasn't, I didn't even know if I'd be glad or sorry . . .

On the third ring, he picked up the phone. "Cantrell," he said crisply. That always made me mad. He wasn't a big-time detective in his Calgary office any more. Why couldn't he just say "hello" like anyone else?

For a second I couldn't make myself answer. I heard him take a deep, impatient breath. "Hello? Who is this?" Another second and he was going to hang up.

"Dad? It's me . . ." I didn't know what I was going to say next, but it didn't matter. I never got the chance to say it, anyway.

"Jared! What do you think you're doing? First I get a call from Mr. Schafer saying that you've had a fist fight with Lance, of all people, then you just up and take off from school in the middle of the afternoon. You just disappear into thin air. You and Lance both. Four hours you've been gone without a trace. Four hours! Do you hear me Jared?" I heard him all right. I was holding the receiver about six inches from my ear but I still heard him, loud and clear.

I waited a few seconds to see if he was done yelling. And I guess he must have finally run out of stored-up mad, because he suddenly calmed down and said the first useful thing since he'd picked up the phone. "Where are you, Jared?"

I swallowed. "In Calgary. Eastside Hospital."

There was a long second of silence on the line. Then, in a tone of voice that I couldn't quite classify, but that wasn't pure anger any more, Dad said, "Hospital? Red, what happened? Are you all right?"

Before I could answer, there was a sudden loud clank, as if somebody had banged the receiver against something hard.

"Hi-eee?" a shrill voice interrupted. "How are you-oo?" High-pitched giggles and more clanks. "My turn! My turn!"

No, please! Not the Willmore twins. Not now of all times. But it was them all right. Other kids' mothers spent a lot of money buying their kids electronic toys but not Sherrie Willmore. She just let Alberta Government Telephones supply her kids with entertainment . . .

I heard Dad give a roar that made me jump even seventy miles away. "Cissy! You put that phone down or I'll . . ." he began, but a sweet, little voice interrupted.

"I'm not Cissy. I'm Cindy. And I'll tell my mommy that you yelled at me . . ." More clanks. It sounded like someone was banging two metal lids together.

"Jared, can you still hear me?" Dad bellowed, obviously deciding that volume was his only weapon. "Are you all right?"

"Old Macdonald had a farm, ee-i-ee-i . . ."

"Eastside Hospital, Dad. Just get here."

I didn't know if he had heard me or not. But if he hadn't, he was out of luck because I'd just run out of time, money and patience, all at the same time. I hung up.

It wasn't until I was back in the waiting room that it occurred to me that I'd just given Dad an order. That was a first. Probably it would be a last, too, when he caught up to me, but the way things were going right now I didn't really care.

21

I walked toward the desk, planning to see if I could get any information from the nurse. Then something made me turn and glance down the long hall that led to all those treatment rooms. And that's when I spotted him, the red-haired intern. I took off after him. He sure did walk fast. I was almost running by the time I got close enough to get his attention without getting the attention of everyone else in the whole hospital. "Hey, uh, Dr. Melvin . . ."

He turned around and gave me kind of a blank look and it occurred to me that he probably hadn't slept in a long time. He sure looked like he could use a nap.

"I was wondering about . . ." I began, but suddenly he snapped his fingers and pointed at me. "Your friend, the dark kid with the cut hand . . . ?"

I nodded.

"He's fine. Everything's under control. He's just waiting for the plastic surgeon to come down and . . ."

"Plastic surgeon?" I interrupted, still not sure that he had me connected with the right patient.

Dr. Melvin laughed. "Don't panic. He's not getting a nose job. Plastic surgeons do a lot of the delicate work on hands—things like putting fingers back on people who insist on cleaning the grass out of their lawn mowers while the motor's running. And, in your friend's case, repairing the nerves and tendons that were cut."

Cut nerves and tendons? Something Lance had said echoed through my mind. "I can't close it . . ." What if? And a picture flashed across my mind. That rainy night before things had started going crazy. Lance's hand holding the pencil and making the eagle so real that I was sure that if I touched it, I'd feel feathers . . .

I looked up into the intern's cheerful face. "*Can* they repair cut nerves and tendons?" I asked.

He nodded. "It's amazing what they can do these days. Of course, it depends on the degree of damage but, from what I could see, it looks like he'll regain most of the function. Maybe not quite as good as it was. He could have a little trouble with really fine co-ordination, but," he smiled, "he should be okay unless he's a violinist."

I could tell that he figured he was giving me good news. But I wasn't so sure. "Or an artist?" I asked in a low voice.

Dr. Melvin gave me a thoughtful look but he didn't ask any questions. "An artist could have some problems to overcome," he said slowly. Then he changed the subject. "There's no reason you shouldn't stay with him while he's waiting for Dr. McKelvey. Somebody will kick you out when they're ready to work on him."

I didn't have any doubts about that.

He led me to a room and opened the door. "See you around, Red," he said, grinning. I wondered how he had happened to come up with that lucky guess . . .

It was pretty interesting in that room. Lots of complicated equipment I'd have liked to explore a little.

But I felt like a little kid in a china store — if I touched *anything* I'd be in *big* trouble.

Lance was lying there with his eyes closed. His hand was wrapped in a clean bandage and an IV tube was plugged into the back of his left hand. They had taken off his blood-soaked clothes and he was wearing a funny-looking pair of pajama bottoms with little yellow flowers on them. I figured that sticking him in that get-up had probably hurt worse than anything else they'd done to him so far.

At least he didn't look as bad as he had when I brought him in here. Now he mostly just looked tired. And he wasn't alone in that. I almost wished they'd get me a pair of those pajamas and let me lie down too.

Then, gawking around and not looking where I was going, as usual, I kicked into the bottom of some sort of metal cabinet. The clang probably woke up the patients in the morgue. It woke up Lance, anyhow. He opened his eyes. "Hey, Klutz, who let you in?" he asked, not doing a very good job of hiding the fact he was glad to see me.

"Dr. Melvin," I said.

Lance nodded. "Yeah, he's okay. Better than that big nurse. I thought she was gonna slug you if you gave her any lip . . ."

"Me too, and that would have made three times I'd got slugged today."

"Three strikes and you're out," Lance said. I don't know what was so funny about that, but we looked at each other and started to laugh. It felt good.

But a minute later Lance's face turned serious. "They call my dad?" he asked.

"Yeah. At least, the nurse was going to. I gave her the number."

Lance nodded and neither of us said anything for a while. Then he looked up and asked, "You talk to the cops yet?"

The cops? For a minute my mind was a total blank. Why would I want to talk to the cops? Then, all of a sudden, the truth hit me like a ton of bricks. I might not want to talk to them but they sure would want to talk to me. It was just a little matter of being smack in the middle of a drug deal that turned into a kidnapping that turned into a knifing. Cops found that sort of conversation real interesting. Then I remembered that phone call the nurse had made. Now I had a pretty good idea why she had been talking to Sgt. Bernelli, whoever he was. I sighed. "No, not yet. But I think they're probably on their way . . ."

Lance turned a little so he could see me better. "Tell them the truth, Red," he said, dead serious. "You didn't do anything illegal and there's no way you can be in any trouble," he paused and then added, "with them." And, I knew he was thinking about how much trouble I was going to be in with Dad. That was a subject I had been avoiding even thinking about. Lance went on, "Just don't turn hero on me and try to cover up for me or anything stupid like that."

I didn't understand what he was talking about. For a minute I thought they must have frozen his brain as well as his hand. Randy was the guy in trouble here, not me — or Lance.

"Cover up for you?" I said incredulously. "Hey man, what do you think? They're gonna throw the book at you for letting Randy cut you up? You're the victim, dummy. The good guy. The cops are going to congratulate you."

Lance shifted position restlessly. That table didn't look any too comfortable. He gave me a long look before he shot me down with one sentence. "You think they're gonna congratulate me for dealin' grass at school for Randy?" he asked, his voice soft.

I realized then that, somehow, with everything

else that had happened this afternoon, I had managed to push that scene with Lance and Don Watson to the back of my mind, put it on "hold," and forget about it. But now it was back, the memory pouring out, boiling over like a pot left simmering on the stove too long. And I couldn't get away from it. Lance, my best friend, had been dealing drugs. I felt like I was living in the re-run of a show I had seen before—and hated. Only last time, it had been Greg, my hero big brother. The past and present were getting all mixed up together into one big, ugly mess.

I guess I must have been staring at Lance as if he had suddenly grown fangs or something. When I finally managed to drag my mind back to the present he was talking to me in a voice that was halfway between angry and pleading. "Hey, come on, Red. Quit lookin' at me like I just joined the Mafia or something. What you walked in on was my first — and only — trip into the dope dealin' business. Honest, Red." Then he looked away from me and added, "Well, I bought some grass from Randy once before that." I didn't say anything and I guess he thought I didn't believe him. His eyes met mine again. "It's the truth, Red. I'm not really into that stuff."

I knew it was the truth. I just wished I could quit seeing Greg when I looked at him. "What'd you do it for, Lance?" I asked, my voice sounding kind of choked. "I mean, the whole business of you and Randy. It just doesn't make any sense."

Lance shrugged. "I don't know why," he said, and from the lost look in his eyes, I believed him. There was a long silence. He looked up at me. "I really don't know. Maybe to get even."

"To get even with your mom?"

"Yeah, her I guess. Everybody."

I didn't say anything. I just sat there staring across the room, wondering what Greg would say he had done it for — if Greg could say anything.

Lance managed to get enough slack in the IV tube to prop himself up with his left hand and look at me square on. "Red, what is it with you, anyhow? Look, I know the dope bit was stupid." He sighed. "The stupidest thing I've pulled in my whole life. But the way you looked at me just now, and the way you looked when you saw me and Watson back at the school. It's like you're taking the whole thing personal.

"It is personal," I said.

"What do you mean?" he asked, his voice puzzled.

"I just don't want you to end up like my brother," I said, wondering if my voice sounded as strange to him as it did to me. I also wondered how it was suddenly so easy to talk about what I'd never been able to tell him before.

"You don't have a brother," he said — no, asked — his eyes full of questions.

"I did."

"He died?" Lance asked almost in a whisper.

"No. He wasn't that lucky . . ." And then I was telling him. Telling him the whole story that had always seemed too hard to start. Now I couldn't get it stopped. Not until I got to the end.

Lance just lay there looking at me for a long time after I stopped talking. Finally he asked the question I knew would be coming. "How come you never told me?"

There was only one answer, another question. I asked it. "How come you never told me about your mother?"

The silence that fell between us then might have lasted a long time, but the footsteps outside the door interrupted it. The door opened and a nurse and a doctor came in. Dr. McKelvey, I presumed. He was a big, round-faced guy who looked more like he should be a farmer than a plastic surgeon. "Sorry I kept you waiting so long, Lance. You all froze up good and solid?"

Lance nodded. The doctor turned to look at me. "I was just leaving," I said, being a fast learner. Just as I reached for the door handle, there was a sharp knock and the door swung open. Two uniformed policemen stood in the doorway.

"Excuse me, doctor," the tall one said. "We were told we might find," he consulted a piece of paper, "a Lance Ducharme — he pronounced the 'ch' like it was spelled instead of like it's supposed to be, with a 'sh' sound — and a Jared Cantrell." The Jared came out totally unrecognizable but he got the last part right so I couldn't say, "Never heard of him" and split like I wanted to.

Dr. McKelvey didn't look any too pleased with the interruption. "This one's Ducharme and you can't have him until I get through with him. If that one's Cantrell, take him, and all of you get out of here so I can get this job done."

22

Well, no matter what Lance had said, there was no way I was about to serve him up like a lamb to the slaughter. I knew he'd been telling the truth about this whole drug business just being a way of rebelling against Anne-Marie and I didn't figure it had anything to do with what the cops needed to know. I thought that if I was careful I could tell the story without letting him in for any more trouble than he already had — although it did occur to me that, even if he ended up in jail, he'd still be better off here than as Anne-Marie's prisoner in Nashville or somewhere.

Either I'd lucked into the meanest pair of cops on the Calgary force, or else I must have been giving off guilty vibes all over the place, because they sure weren't buying my story. For the third time, the short, heavy-set one asked me how Randy "just happened" to pick us up and take us hostage. And I gave my third, slightly-altered version of how we were just walking along, minding our own business — but, like I said before, I'm a lousy liar and the story was even sounding a little weak to me . . .

The cop cut me off in mid-sentence. "Listen, punk. Don't get cute with me. You've got that story worked up till you could sell used cars with it, but I'm not looking for transportation so you'd better run it by me one more time. Now, how's it go again?" he asked sarcastically. "You and your buddy in there, two innocent little country boys who wouldn't know a joint from a bale of hay, were just walkin' along . . ." Suddenly he grabbed me by the shirt front and jerked me up on my toes. "Come on, kid, get serious . . ." he began, but he never finished the sentence because the door burst open behind him. Over his shoulder I caught a glimpse of my dad coming charging into the room.

He was out of uniform, wearing jeans and a plaid shirt, but that didn't matter. Everything about him still spelled "authority." He paused in the doorway, his eyes sweeping the room, taking in the whole scene and then coming to rest on me. In three strides, he crossed the room and was beside me. And if the cop hadn't still been holding onto me, I know I would have backed up. These two strange cops had been hassling me for half an hour but they still hadn't begun to scare me the way my own dad did.

But, amazingly, it wasn't me that Dad lit into; it was the big cop. "Let go of him," Dad ordered, and the cop's hand dropped to his side before he had time to wonder what this guy thought he was doing, giving him orders. Dad has that effect on people. When he says "jump" they ask "how high?" on the way up. But now the cop reacted.

"Hey, who do you think you are . . . ?" he began but, again, Dad took control away from him.

"You don't remember me, McMillan?" he said, more than asked, and the cop stopped glaring and took a long, puzzled look at Dad. Then recognition flashed across his face.

"Inspector Cantrell. I didn't know you were back on the force. We heard you were top gun in some little town now . . ." I took a closer look at McMillan.

Then I remembered who he was. Sergeant McMillan. He'd worked out of the same headquarters as Dad did when he was a detective here. In fact, Dad had been his boss.

"You heard right," Dad said. "My stake in this is personal."

"Personal?" The sergeant sounded halfway between irritated and curious. I tried to remember what Dad had ever said about what kind of guy McMillan was. A good cop, he'd said that. But pig-headed. I think they had respected each other but never really been friends. Too much alike, maybe.

"Yeah, real personal. That's my son you're leaning on."

McMillan looked at me, then back to Dad, and I could practically see the wheels going around in his head. Cantrell's son, eh? But he'd already had one son mixed up in a big, messy drug investigation — the worst scandal to hit the force in a long time. And since that kid was definitely in no shape to be running around loose, Cantrell must have a whole string of juvenile delinquents on his hands.

Dad finished his sentence. "And I'd appreciate it if you'd just back off long enough to let me have a few minutes to sort this all out with him."

McMillan looked at Dad. Then he looked at me. I could see him getting ready to refuse — to take this chance to pull rank on his old boss. I knew that he'd decided I was guilty as sin, though of what I wasn't sure, and I didn't think he was about to let me off the hook, even because of my dad. Or maybe especially because of my dad.

The two of them stood there for what seemed like a long while, measuring each other. I knew that, as far as actual police authority went, Dad was out of his territory — and out of luck. But there are different kinds of authority and Dad has the kind that comes with the person, not the position. The sergeant's eyes shifted. He looked at his partner and found bored neutrality. That guy had never been pushing like McMillan. As far as I could see, getting home in time for dinner was probably the biggest issue on his mind right then.

McMillan nodded. "Okay, Cantrell, he's yours — for now. An RCMP car is on its way to the cabin to pick up this Randy Borowski, who is supposedly" — he stressed that word "supposedly" and gave me a fishy look like he thought I'd invented the whole thing — "locked in the cellar there. We'll check and see what they found out and then, we'll be back."

Dad nodded. "Thanks, Sergeant," he said. "I'll see that you get the story straight." And he meant that too. However bad the truth might be, he'd see that it was told. That was just the way he did things.

McMillan gave me one more sour look and then he and his partner turned and walked away. I watched them go, almost regretfully. I hadn't exactly been enjoying our discussion but, still, whatever kind of slimy little hood they thought I was, it didn't really matter to me. They were strangers. I didn't care a whole lot what they thought of me. But with Dad it was a whole different story . . .

I turned back toward him. It took all I had to meet his eyes but I managed it. I was expecting to see anger, disappointment, accusation — but most of what I saw was concern.

"Come on, Red, sit down," he said, his voice low, but I just stood there in a daze, staring at him. His patience wore thin fast, as usual. "I said, 'Sit down,' " he barked in his "giving-orders" voice. In spite of myself, I jumped. I don't know what was wrong with me. Being yelled at by him sure wasn't anything new. But I guess I must have been more strung out than I realized. I sat down. And tried to stop my hands from shaking. I knew that if he yelled at me again I was likely to start bawling right there in front of everybody in that waiting room.

But he didn't yell. He didn't say anything for what seemed like a long time. I looked up at him and, as I did, his hand reached down and squeezed my shoulder. "It's okay, Red," he said gently. "Just take it easy. Everything's going to be okay." He sat down beside me on the couch and put his arm around me and I knew that he understood how close to falling apart I was right then. It felt like his strong arm around me was what was holding me together.

"Now, just tell me what happened. Slow and easy. First of all, what happened to you? Where are you hurt?"

"Hurt?" I repeated, bewildered. "I'm not hurt." Then I realized that he was staring at my blood-spattered jacket. "Oh, that's not my blood. It's Lance's. But he's okay — I think. The doctor's working on him now. It's a pretty bad cut. He never should have tried to grab that knife. Not with Randy freaked out the way he was . . ." I was talking fast, trying to explain everything in a hurry when Dad finally stopped me.

"Red," he cut in, his voice not angry but calm and firm. "Try starting at the beginning."

I looked up at him, confused. Where was the beginning? Did the whole thing start today or ten years ago? One thing was for sure, though. The beginning wasn't where I'd started in the story I gave McMillan. For a minute, I wondered if I should try giving the same story to Dad. But if I lied to Dad, he would know. It's always been that way. And I also realized that even if he would believe a lie, I didn't want to start lying to him now. Right now, I needed to trust somebody. And I needed him to trust me just as much.

So I started at the beginning, and I didn't leave out anything. And Dad listened. All the way through, he just listened. Not a single "Why?" or "Didn't you know any better than . . . ?" I could hardly believe that he was really sitting there calmly listening to me, listening to the whole story.

Finally I got to the end and I waited. I waited for him to get mad at me. To tell me how bad I'd messed up. How dumb I had been. But he didn't. He didn't do any of those things. All he did was ask one question. "It that the same story you told those two officers who questioned you?"

Well, if he was only going to ask one question, he'd picked a good one. I shook my head. Now, here it comes, I thought. Now I'm really going to get it for not telling them the whole truth. Dad asked one more question.

"What didn't you tell them?" he asked, his eyes studying my face.

I took a deep breath. "The part about Lance and Don Watson," I said slowly. "And the reason why Randy stopped on the bridge to talk to Lance."

Dad nodded. "I thought it would be something like that," he said quietly. What was he waiting for? Why didn't he yell at me and get if over with? I could take that. I was used to his disapproval. What I couldn't take was waiting for it to come.

"You were trying to cover for Lance," Dad said, and I wasn't sure if it was a question or statement.

I nodded. "Guess you think that was pretty stupid, huh?"

He didn't say anything for a minute. Finally, he shook his head. "No, I don't think it was stupid. I think you got into something you didn't know how to handle and you followed your first instinct which was to protect your friend. That's not so stupid. There are a lot of worse instincts you could have picked."

Then, before I had time to think all that over, he added, "But I don't think it's the right way to leave things. Sgt. McMillan still needs to get the story straight for his records. And if it was up to me, I'd tell him the truth . . . ."

That had to be the gentlest order I'd ever got from Dad. But it was still just that — an order. I didn't see any way to get out of doing what he said, especially since I had to admit that, when it came right down to it, he was dead right. Rearranging stories to tell the cops was definitely not one of my talents. If McMillan had walked back into the room at that exact moment, I'd have been glad to see him just to get the whole mess straightened out and off of my chest — if it hadn't been for one thing: where was it going to leave Lance?

"Yeah, I guess you're right, Dad. But I don't think I can do it."

Dad didn't say anything, just gave me a questioning look and waited.

"It's just not fair to Lance," I said. "He doesn't deserve to come out of this looking like some small-time pusher. Like Randy's partner or something. You know him better than that. He wasn't even thinking straight when he got mixed up in the whole deal in the first place . . . ."

"Red," Dad stopped me, "Did Lance ask you to cover for him?"

Slowly I shook my head. "No," I said miserably, "He said to tell it like it was."

Dad nodded. "Okay then. Don't you think you owe it to him to do that?"

I gave up. "All right," I sighed. "I'll tell Sgt. Mc-Millan."

Dad's face softened a little and the wrinkles at the corners of his mouth looked like the beginning of a smile. "Good. You can straighten it out as soon as he gets back. And, by the way, Red, give the Calgary police force a little credit, eh? A fifteen-year-old who almost sold a couple of joints but ended up in the hospital because he jumped in and saved his friend from getting knifed isn't going to be their first choice to send to Spy Hill — especially not when they hear the character reference he's going to get from ex-Inspector Cantrell."

It felt like Dad had just picked up the whole world and taken if off my shoulders. "Thanks, Dad," was all I could think of to say. But it was enough. He put his arm around me and squeezed. He was strong — strong and dependable. I had almost forgotten that. Somewhere along the way I'd got it all mixed up with being hard and unyielding . . .

For the first time all day, I was beginning to feel like something might turn out right.

Then Dad gave me a puzzled look. "I've just got one more question," he said.

"Yeah, Dad?"

"You said you drove Lance here in Randy's Corvette?"

I nodded, not sure what this was leading up to.

"Where did you ever learn to drive a car like that?"

Well, I didn't really know what to say but since we were into telling the whole truth . . .

I shrugged. "Oh, I don't know exactly. Somewhere between the cabin and Calgary, I guess. With a few finishing touches on Sixteenth Avenue."

Dad got the strangest look on his face and I began to wonder if he was going to get mad at me after all. But he began to laugh. He laughed so loud that some of the other people in the room turned to glare at us. Obviously you are not supposed to find anything funny in a hospital. Finally he stopped laughing enough to be able to talk. "You really did that? You just figured it out as you went along?" I nodded and he started laughing again. "You crazy kid! You crazy, red-headed son-of-a-gun! If you live to grow up you're going to be quite a guy." He reached over and grabbed me in a bear hug that almost squashed me. And I just sat there, suffocating and grinning like an idiot.

"Excuse me," said a voice, and I came back to reality, in the form of Sgt. McMillan. "The RCMP picked up this Borowski kid at the cabin so that part of the story checks out," he said, looking kind of disappointed, I thought. "Now, if we could get the rest of it straight," he added, with a stern look at me. "You want to be in on this lieutenant?" he asked, sounding a lot more respectful than he had earlier.

Dad gave me a long look and this time I didn't find it so hard to return that look. Then he shook his head. "No, thanks, sergeant. My son doesn't need any help. I'll get myself a coffee and wait over here." And there was something about the way he walked away, looking unconcerned that made me feel anything but deserted . . .

Telling the truth didn't turn out to be so hard after all. In fact, compared to lying, it was downright easy. It was a lot less complicated to remember what happened when you weren't trying to make it up as you went along.

When I got to the end, for the first time, Sgt. McMillan looked at me with something less than hostility. He made a final note in his little book and then looked up. "All right," he said. "That pretty well matches the story Borowski told the RCMP. We'll wait until the Ducharme kid is feeling better to talk to him. Anyway, it looks like you and he are pretty well clear of any charges. We may need to call on you again when Borowski's case comes up in court. Looks like he's going to be pretty busy hiring lawyers. The charges against him read like a dictionary of legal terms — kidnap, wounding with intent, trafficking . . . you name it.

"Well, thanks for your co-operation," he added, almost pleasantly. Dad had wandered over with his coffee now and McMillan nodded to him. "Nice to see you again, inspector," he said as he and his partner turned to leave. "You, too, McMillan," Dad said. I was just going to tell him about my discussion with the sergeant when the desk nurse came over.

"Sorry to bother you," she said to me, "But I've been trying to get hold of your friend's father. He doesn't answer at the number you gave me and we've had the RCMP at Alderton checking his house and a few of his neighbours but no one seems to know where he is. We really do need to have him come in to sign some papers . . ."

Dad stepped forward. "I think I can find him," he said, showing her his police ID. "Give me a couple of hours."

The nurse nodded. "Thank you. I'd really appreciate that." She walked away and I gave Dad a questioning look.

He explained. "When you and Lance disappeared I didn't know what to think so I went to see if Mike had any ideas. He told me about the custody hearing tomorrow and he said that Lance had been acting strange lately so it was possible he had just taken off and that you'd ended up going with him. He figured that if you two were looking for a place to hole-up for a while you might have headed for The Valley . . ."

"I wish we had," I said, mainly to myself, thinking of how peaceful it was back there.

Dad went on. "So Mike's taken a horse and gone back there looking for you two. If he didn't find you he was supposed to meet me at our place. But . . ."

Dad's face softened into a half-embarrassed grin, ". . after your fairly definite instructions on the phone, I didn't think I'd better wait."

I didn't bite on that so he went on. "Anyway, Mike should be on his way back by now. I'll take the four-wheel drive and go meet him and bring him down here. I'll be back as soon as I can." He gave my shoulder a final squeeze and started for the door. But then he stopped and turned to look back at me. "You want to come with me, son?" he asked. And I almost jumped at the chance. For the first time in three years, I really wanted to be with my dad. To get out of this stinking hospital and drive away with him. Forget today ever happened and just be a kid again. Let him make the decisions and solve the problems.

But even as "yes" was running through my mind, I knew it wasn't that simple. I guess for everybody there has to come a time when you suddenly realize that, no matter how much you want to stop the clock, stay a kid, and leave all the serious stuff to the grown-ups, you just can't do it any more. Because now your problems aren't ones that they can solve for you. No one else can do it for you. I guessed that time had come for me now.

I stood there alone, in the middle of the room, with Dad's eyes on me, waiting for my answer. I shook my head. "I'd better stay here," I said. "Lance will expect me to be around when the doctor gets done with him. I think he could use some company."

Dad smiled. "That's what I thought you'd say," he said, and he gave me one last look before he turned away. I wasn't sure what all was in that look. I almost thought some of it could have been pride.

23

I looked at my watch for the tenth time in as many minutes. 9:20 now. It had been over two hours since the plastic surgeon had gone in there. What was he doing anyhow? Amputating at the elbow?

I couldn't stand it any longer. I walked up to the desk and asked the nurse if she knew what was happening. She checked through some papers. "Hmmm, here it is. Ducharme. Oh, he's been done for a long time. They took him up to the ward about half an hour ago. You can go on up. Room 501. Elevator's right through there."

Half an hour ago! And all that time I'd been pacing around here digesting my fingernails because nobody had bothered to tell me. Real considerate bunch, these hospital people. For two cents I would have punched somebody. But nobody offered me two cents and I didn't know who it was that needed punching so I just stalked off without losing my dignity — until I reached the hall door, gave it a violent push and almost bounced off it before I read the word PULL in big letters . . .

I got off the elevator and looked around. It was the fifth floor, all right. I followed the arrows down the hall and found 501 on the first try. The door was closed. And suddenly I was scared to open it. I was so tired that I was beginning to get light-headed. Today had been so crazy that I found myself wondering if I had imagined everything that had happened. What if, in reality, I was sleepwalking or something? What if I opened the door and walked into a roomful of old ladies in their nightgowns — or even young ladies in their nightgowns?

I reached for the door handle but I pulled my hand back. I really was chicken. Then, a voice behind me made me jump. It was a nurse. "Well, you finally found the place. Your friend's been wondering what happened to you." She smiled. "You are Red, I assume, if my eyes aren't deceiving me." I guess she was just trying to be friendly but I didn't even grin. I was in no mood to have my feathers ruffled.

"Yeah, it's me," I muttered and walked inside.

It was a double room but the other bed was empty and I was glad. The last thing I wanted right then was some stranger gawking at us. At first I thought Lance was asleep. He was lying there real still and stillness isn't his usual state when he's awake. Then I realized that he didn't have much choice about lying still. With his left hand still connected with the IV and his right encased in a shiny, new, white cast, there weren't a whole lot of moves he could make.

When I walked over to the bed he opened his eyes and turned his head to look at me. His eyes and hair looked startlingly dark against the white sheets but his face didn't look quite as pale as it had.

"Paleface get lost in corridors?" he asked lazily, giving me a kind of sleepy grin. I stared at him, wondering how he could be acting so relaxed when he'd been so strung-out a couple of hours ago. I decided he must be about half-high on pain-killers or something. Whatever it was, just being with him was starting to calm me down, too. I flopped into a chair.

"Don't ask, Geronimo," I groaned. "You wouldn't believe me if I told you. For a while I was beginning to think they must have hauled you off to an operating room and installed a brain while they had the chance."

Lance laughed. "No, but Dr. McKelvey had me scared for a minute."

"How come?"

"Well, after they promised they were just gonna freeze my hand and fix it, right there in emergency, he suddenly asked me how old I was. When I told him he started talking about waiting until tomorrow and knocking me right out to work on me."

I could see why Lance hadn't liked that idea. Like he'd said about Randy's driving once, things he couldn't control scared him. And when you're unconscious you can't control much.

"What's your age got to do with it?" I asked.

"That's what I wanted to know. McKelvey said kids my age are usually too skittish to do much with when they're awake."

"Skittish?" I repeated. I'd heard a lot of colourful language, some not repeatable, used to describe teenagers but that was a new one. "Sounds like he was talking about a horse," I said.

"That's what I thought."

"So, how'd you talk him out of it?"

Lance looked up and grinned. "I told him I was well-broke and gentle."

"What'd he say?"

"He laughed. It turned out he's got a farm just outside Calgary and he raises some Quarter Horses, so he knew what I meant. We got along real good. For about the first hour, that is . . ."

"And then?"

Lance grinned sheepishly. "And then I started getting skittish."

We both laughed. Then Lance changed the subject. "I wasn't figuring on all this," he said, his eyes
sweeping the hospital room. "They're gonna keep
me here for a couple of days, the nurse said. I thought
they were just gonna sew me up and then let me go
home . . ." That last word came out kind of hoarse
and his voice trailed off. Then his face clouded over.
"I guess it don't matter much when I get out now . . ."
The sentence didn't sound finished but I was afraid
that I knew what he was thinking. If he stuck to his
decision to go with his mother, "home" was going to
take on a whole new meaning for him. Where he
would be going wouldn't be home at all . . . I didn't
want to start thinking about that. I couldn't right
now . . .

I realized I was sweating. I didn't know how much
of it was from tension and how much was from the
fact that the hospital was even more over-heated
than Alderton School usually is. Anyway, since I felt
like I should say something, the temperature was a
nice, unemotional topic, I thought.

"What are they trying to do in this place, heat the
germs to death? It's boiling in here!"

Lance gave me sort of a sarcastic look. "So, why
don't you try takin' your jacket off, genius?"

I looked down at myself and was half-surprised to
discover that I was still wearing my denim jacket.
Maybe Lance had a point there. I stood up and took
it off.

It really looked like I'd worn it through a war, I
decided as I folded it over, getting ready to lay it on
the extra chair. But, as I did, something heavy and
gold slipped out of the pocket and landed silently on
the bed. I knew what it was. And for the third time
since I'd had it, the thought crossed my mind. This
is definitely not the time to give it back. It was the
last thing Lance needed to see right now. But I was

too late. Before I could pick it up, he raised his head to see what it was. When he jumped like he'd touched a hot branding iron, I knew that he had recognized the St. Christopher's Medal. That sea of chemical calm he had been floating on suddenly got hit by a hurricane. Drugged or not, he was wide-awake now. Instinctively, he tried to reach out for the medal with his cast-covered right hand, but sudden pain tensed his face and he caught his breath as his head fell back on the pillow.

He lay there with his eyes closed for a few seconds and, when he opened them again, I held the medal out where he could reach it with his left hand. He took it and held it a while, looking at it. Then he looked up at me, a question in his eyes.

I nodded. "Yeah, I picked it up the night you threw it away," I said, feeling unreasonably guilty for having it, somehow. "I thought you'd just lost it. I've been carrying it around, meaning to give it back to you ever since." It was the truth but it felt almost like a lie, like I'd stolen something valuable and was trying to cover up.

Lance nodded. "So that's why I couldn't find it," he said softly. When I didn't say anything he went on. "Yeah, I went back looking for it after you were gone that night. I threw it away because I never wanted to see it — or her, again. Because she was alive when she wasn't supposed to be . . . And then," he said softly, "when it was gone I had to try and find it again. A real gutless wonder, huh? But that was when I only knew that she was alive. Before I knew that she was going to fight for custody! Suddenly, his eyes blazed. "Take it," he said, in a low, ragged voice. "Just get it out of here. Throw it away someplace where I'll never find it." His voice was rising. "I don't want it!" He held it out to me with a movement so violent that he almost jerked the IV tube out of his hand. He was shaking, on the edge of losing the control he'd been fighting all afternoon to hold onto.

I took the medal and held it, warm and heavy in my hand. I thought about what Lance had said. About how he'd gone back to find it. And I thought about hate, and love — and how hard they were to tell apart. Then I shook my head. "Sorry, Lance. I can't do that. If you want to throw it away again, I guess you've got the right. I won't try to stop you. But I won't do it for you."

He didn't say anything but I could feel his eyes burning into me as I carefully wound the broken chain around the medal and laid it on the table beside the bed.

I don't know what either one of us would have said or done next; things were getting kind of tense in that room. But we didn't have the chance to find out because the silence was broken by the sound of footsteps outside the door. The kind of footsteps that don't fit into the rubber-soled hospital world. These sounded like high heels — and whoever was wearing them was running . . .

The door burst open and Anne-Marie was standing there, framed in the doorway. I couldn't take my eyes off of her. It was like a meteorite had just flashed into the room. She had on a silver and turquoise dress that glittered when she moved, high-heeled silver boots that came to her knees, long, dangly, silver earings, and her hair seemed even longer and curlier than ever . . .

And I'd thought she was beautiful before! Now she looked like she had just walked onstage. Suddenly what Lance had said about the concert being tonight registered and I realized that she probably *had* just walked onstage. I glanced at my watch. 9:35. The concert wasn't supposed to start until 8:30. It couldn't be over yet. What was she doing here?

Lance turned to see what I was looking at then

and I sensed, more than saw, his whole body go tense. Still nobody said a word. I didn't know what was going to happen but I did know that this was a scene I didn't belong in. Even though I hadn't moved, Lance must have been able to read the "getting out of there" vibrations in my mind. He looked right at me and said in a low voice that only I could hear, "Don't leave, Red."

He couldn't have stopped me. There was no way he could have reached out and grabbed me with either hand. But I got the message — if he had pointed a gun at my head, the message couldn't have come through any stronger. Anyway, I don't think Anne-Marie even realized I was sitting there in the chair on the far side of the bed — or, if she did, I didn't matter to her any more than the furniture did right then. Because in that whole room she was seeing only one thing — Lance.

Suddenly she was running across the room. "Oh, Lance," she said, and it was hardly more than a whisper, "I was so scared . . ." And then, she was standing by the bed, leaning over, searching her son's face. Looking down at him with those fantastic dark eyes. I tried to read what was in those eyes. Fear, for one thing. And that was the first time I'd ever seen Anne-Marie afraid of anything. But there was something else, too. A softness that hadn't been there before. Then, all at once, I understood why Anne-Marie couldn't just back off, go back to her own world, and stop messing up her son's life. All along, I'd thought she was out to prove something. To prove to the world — and to herself — that, not only could she make it as a star, she could make it as a mother too. But now, watching the way she looked at him, I knew that I'd been wrong. That wasn't why she wanted Lance. Not now, anyway. She wanted him because she really did love him.

"I've been in every hospital in town trying to find you. I didn't know where you were, how badly hurt you were . . ." She reached out then and gently brushed Lance's too-long hair back out of his eyes. And, at her touch, Lance looked up at her. And the eyes were the same. The image of his mother's. Even the softness was the same. Ten years of pain and bitterness got lost in that look.

It made me think of one of those times you read about in war stories when, just for a few minutes, armies stop tearing each other to pieces and call a truce. Stop being enemies and remember that, when it comes right down to it, they're all just people. And, right then, Anne-Marie and Lance had forgotten that they were at war with each other and remembered what they had never really stopped being. Two people who loved and needed each other.

Lance was just a kid. A kid who'd had to grow up too fast and be too strong and too tough too soon. A scared, hurt kid who wanted his mother to be there.

And Anne-Marie was just a mother. Not a glitter-covered picture on an album cover. Now, except for being about twice as beautiful, she was like any other mother, worrying over her hurt kid.

She shook her head as her eyes took in the IV, the cast on his hand, and her voice was gentle when she spoke again. "You poor kid. You're so messed up. And it's all my fault. But I'm going to make it up to you, Lance. From now on, things are going to be different. You'll be with me . . ."

She didn't get a chance to finish that sentence. It was as if those last few words had broken the spell. The beautiful queen had turned into the wicked witch. Lance jerked away from her like she'd slapped him. The lonely little boy was gone, changed into a half-grown tiger cub that was all claws and ready to spit and growl and scratch whenever she came near him. "What are you doing here?" he asked, in a voice that was all ice. "Why aren't you out there where you belong, entertaining your fans?"

Lance was street-fighting. Using words instead of fists and boots but fighting just as dirty. Out to hurt. To pick his opponent's weak spot and hammer away at it. To re-open old wounds. And if he had practised for years, he couldn't have picked any better words to do it, to remind Anne-Marie of where her priorities had always been. Then it struck me that he probably *had* been practising for years — nearly ten of them. Ten years of never being able to forget the choice his mother had made. Her career. Her fans. She had picked them over her son once. So, why should it be any different now? Just because Lance was hurt?

The words did their job. Just for a second, I could see the pain flicker across Anne-Marie's face. And for the first time, I felt sorry for her. Lance was playing pretty rough. But I still couldn't blame him for saying what he had. Maybe it was his turn to be on the giving end of the hurting for a while. He'd sure done his share of taking it. But I wasn't so sure he could hurt Anne-Marie without hurting himself just as much. No matter how hard he tried, he wasn't going to be able to kill the love he still had for her. He and Anne-Marie were a part of each other, and nothing was going to change that.

Then, for some crazy reason, this morning's science lesson suddenly flashed through my mind. Magnetism, Opposites attract but likes repel . . . I wondered what that had to do with anything. But, as I sat watching the two of them there, so close together and, at the same time so far apart, I realized it wasn't so crazy . . .

Lance and Anne-Marie were likes — so much alike you could have matched them up in a crowd of a

million people. But it was more than looks. It was
feelings. That combination of toughness and sensi-
tivity that they both had. They were survivors. They
got hurt but they healed fast and kept on fighting.
But maybe they healed too fast. Maybe it was like
the vet had told me once, when Pepper had run a
sharp stick into her chest. If you weren't careful, a
deep wound like that would heal from the outside,
cover with scar tissue and look okay. Inside, though,
it wouldn't be healed at all . . .

When Anne-Marie answered him, she was cool,
composed. But I wondered what she was feeling like
inside. "I'm here because I care what happens to
you . . ." she began, but Lance didn't let her finish
that sentence either.

"Yeah, sure," he burst out bitterly. "How could I
have forgot about how much you cared about me?
Maybe because you haven't been around to remind
me for a few years, huh?"

He might just as well have been hitting her with
his fists — maybe he would have if he could. But he
was beating her with words instead. And she stood
there and took it. "Lance," she said, her voice low
but still under control, "You'll never know how sorry I am about those years, but there's nothing I can
do to change them now. All I can do is promise that
from now on . . ."

"Oh, that's great. You did such a good job on my
past that now you want to start in on my future.
And what are you gonna do for my present? Borrow
Randy's knife and try for my heart?"

It took a lot of stored up pain to come out with
something like that. It amazed me that Lance had
been carrying that kind of hurt around all this time
without it ever showing. But, what amazed me even
more was how much Anne-Marie could take. If anybody had talked to me the way Lance had talked to

her, I'd have either slugged them or started bawling
— maybe both. But not her. I saw her swallow hard
and then, hurt but still proud, she said, "Okay, Lance.
We're not getting anywhere this way. I'll talk to you
tomorrow, when you've cooled down some."

She turned to go but Lance stopped her. "No, wait,"
he said, his voice calm but cold. "Since you're here
anyway, there's something I've got to talk to you
about."

Slowly she turned back toward the bed, her face
half-hopeful, half-wary. I could see that she desper-
ately wanted to hear what he had to say but, at the
same time, she was afraid to hear any more. "What
is it, Lance?" she asked cautiously.

"About the custody hearing . . ." he began, and it
sounded like those words almost choked him.

Anne-Marie stopped him, the gentleness back in
her voice, "You don't have to worry about that
now. There's no hurry. We'll get it postponed until
you're . . ."

"No," Lance said. "Not postponed. Called off. For
good. Forever."

Anne-Marie's voice suddenly sounded tired, but
her face was set and stubborn as she answered.
"Lance, please don't start on that again. I don't care
what you think you want. I want what's best for
you. And now, especially after what's happened
today, there's no way I'm going to let . . ."

Lance cut her off. "There's no point in having a
hearing if I've already agreed to go with you, is
there?"

It took a couple of seconds for the full meaning of
that to hit Anne-Marie. She stood there staring down
at Lance, her eyes unbelieving.

"What did you say?" she asked, and it was almost
a whisper.

"You heard me," he said. "Call off the hearing

and I'll go with you." He paused and lay looking up at his mother, waiting for an answer. But at first she didn't answer, and the silence of those few seconds seemed to last for years. It was Lance who finally broke it and I could tell he was getting scared. Scared that his plan wasn't going to work and that he still might have to watch Mike destroyed in court. "I'll tell Dad that I want to go with you. He won't fight you for custody if he thinks I'd rather be with you." Lance's voice was hoarse now, on the edge of breaking, and pleading and angry at the same time. "Come on, I'm making it easy for you. You get what you want if you promise to let me do it my way."

Anne-Marie gave him a long, wondering look. Then, as cautious as a soldier stepping out into a mine field, she asked, "And what is your way, Lance?"

He swallowed and took a couple of deep breaths and I wondered if Anne-Marie could see past the defiance in his eyes to realize how close the tears were. But when he started talking again, his voice was under control. "I'll go live with you," he said, and paused to let the words sink in. "But I go from here. From the hospital. Day after tomorrow, when they let me out of here, if you want me, you come and get me. Pick me up here and we go straight to Nashville — or wherever it is you want to go." The way he said it, it sounded like he didn't much care if it was Nashville or Siberia she had in mind.

Anne-Marie shook her head, bewildered. "But what about all your stuff? Clothes? Books? Whatever you want to take with you. And your horse. There's plenty of room on the acreage. We can get a trailer and take him along . . ."

"No," Lance said. "Spider belongs here. On the ranch. With room to run. Free. He'd be better off dead than stuck in some little two-acre pasture outside Nashville . . ." I wasn't sure it was just the horse he was thinking about when he said that. But before I had time to think about it, I heard my name come up. "You can go out to the ranch and pick up some clothes for me. Red'll go with you."

I felt a protest rising in my mind. Red was not going anywhere with her. But I didn't say anything. Right then, as far as those two were concerned, I might as well have not existed. And I was just as glad. This was one conversation I wanted to stay out of.

Anne-Marie was still looking doubtful. "But why, Lance? Why the big deal about not going back to the ranch? I don't understand."

Lance turned his head restlessly on the pillow and I realized that, on top of everything else that was piling up on top of him right now, being trapped in that bed must be driving him crazy. As long as I'd known him, whenever something bugged Lance he ran or rode fast or piled into some hard, physical job to let off steam. But now, with the tension building up inside him like a time bomb ready to explode, he couldn't do anything but lie there and feel it build . . .

"No," he said to Anne-Marie, his voice rising a little. "You don't understand. You don't understand me at all. If you did you wouldn't have to ask why. But there's one thing you'd better understand. If I ever go home again, back to the ranch, there's no way I'll ever just get in your car and drive away with you. I couldn't do it. But I've made up my mind to go now and I'll do it. From here." He propped himself up with his left hand and looked her straight in the eye. "But if I once go home, it doesn't matter what any judge says I've gotta do, the only way you'll get me away from there is to drag me out." He meant every word of that and I think Anne-Marie knew it. She sat silent, and let him finish. "So make up your mind, lady. We're playing by my rules or not at all. Do you want me or don't you?"

If this had been chess, I would have said that Lance had just captured the queen. There was only one answer Anne-Marie could give if she wanted to stay in the game. So Lance had won that much. Even if he'd had to pawn himself to do it.

Anne-Marie tried one more time. "Lance, I didn't want this to turn out . . ." she began, sounding trapped.

Lance didn't back off an inch. "Yes or no?" he demanded.

Their eyes locked. Two high-voltage lines touching in a high wind. Sparking. Smouldering. Burning each other up. At last, it was Anne-Marie who gave in. "Okay," she sighed. "You win. We do it your way."

I wondered how anyone who had just got what she wanted most, won the biggest battle of her life without ever firing a shot, could look so miserable. And I wondered if the fact that she was miserable made Lance feel any better . . .

I might have wondered a lot of other things but, right then, the door burst open and the whole scene changed.

24

Standing there, framed in the doorway, just like Anne-Marie had been a few minutes ago — but not looking anything like a meteorite, even in his turquoise and silver outfit, stood the creep. Jerry, I mean. I don't know if I'd ever heard his last name. If I had, I'd forgotten it, because "creep" suited him so much better. And tonight he was really going to live up to that name.

He stood there, taking in the scene, a sneer on his weasely face. Then he strode over to Anne-Marie. "You stupid little fool. I've been all over town trying to track you down," he snarled. "You'd better have an explanation and it had better be good." He was absolutely furious. I'd never seen anybody so mad. I wondered for a second if he was going to haul off and hit her. I figured that hitting women would be about his speed. But when I turned to look at Anne-Marie, fear was one thing I didn't see in her face.

She tossed her hair back and turned to face him, controlled fury in her every movement. She looked at him in the same way Lance had looked at my prize worms that day in The Valley. With total contempt. "Yeah, Jerry, as a matter of fact, I do have an explanation. And it's plenty good enough for me. I walked into my dressing room at intermission and got a message from a friend, saying that the police have been at her place trying to find my ex-husband to tell him that our son had been cut up in a knife fight. Well, believe it or not, Jerry, that was all the reason I needed to go and try to find out if my kid was alive or dead. And even if I had left the prime minister himself waiting in the audience, it would have been just too bad. Now how's that for a reason, Jerry? Or doesn't that kind of an explanation make sense to you?"

"No," Jerry snarled. "It doesn't make any sense to me. Tonight was your big chance—our big chance. Ten thousand people, Anne-Marie. Ten thousand of your loyal fans. Waiting for the great Anne-Marie Charbonneau to walk out on the stage. To do her part of the show. The part they've been waiting for. And what happens? You don't show up. Five minutes before you're due on stage you just disappear and leave me to explain to those people that they don't count with you. That you suddenly found something more important to do . . .

"I'm left holding the bag while you go chasing off after a kid you haven't seen for ten years. It's a little late to try to pull the 'big mama' act, isn't it Anne-Marie?" He laughed, a mean, unfunny sound. "You really are stupid, you know. You really think the kid could care less about having you around after all this time? You never even thought about that, did you? Oh, no, you didn't think at all. You just blew the biggest break you ever had to rush to the bedside of your poor, hurt baby. And he's hurt real bad, isn't he? A little cut hand. A real life-and-death situation, eh? Why didn't you just send him a band-aid and save everybody a lot of trouble?

"Get serious, Anne-Marie. Your fans aren't gonna put up with that kind of treatment. And I'm not gonna put up with it either . . ."

Finally Jerry slowed down long enough for Anne-

Marie to answer him. And when she answered, the words came out slow and calm, so Jerry didn't miss a one. "Jerry," she said. "You'll never know how little I care whether or not you're going to put up with what I do. It doesn't really matter now, because you and I aren't going to be together from now on."

That shut Jerry up for a minute, and when he started talking again, he wasn't yelling any more. His voice was low and mean. "Aren't you forgetting something, Anne-Marie? Aren't you forgetting what you were when I first found you? Nothing!" He practically spat the word at her. "Nothing but a stragglyhaired little half-breed in somebody else's dress. And if it wasn't for me, you'd still be nothing. I made you what you are and you'd better not ever forget it."

If those last words were supposed to be a threat, it was lost on Anne-Marie. The way she lit into him, I didn't think she was feeling particularly threatened. "Well, I'm real glad you said that, Jerry. Because right now I'm none too proud of what I am. And here I thought all along that I had only myself to blame. But if you're taking all the credit for making me what I am, then you can just get out of my life and I'll have a try at becoming what I should have been . . ."

I don't know if Jerry was bright enough to take that all in or not but it didn't take much of an IQ to figure out that he'd been told off—but good. And he reacted the way that stupid people usually do when they get cornered. If he couldn't beat Anne-Marie mentally, he'd do it physically.

He grabbed her arm. "I don't have to take that from you, you little . . ." he began, but that was as far as he got. Ever since Jerry had burst in through that door, Lance hadn't said a word — not that anyone had given him a chance to get a word in. But even if they had, you get used to the fact that kids aren't invited to take part in adult fights. Just like when you're little and your mom takes you shopping, look but don't touch. But now it seemed that this had suddenly become Lance's fight, too.

His voice slashed through the air, stopping Jerry in mid-sentence. "Leave her alone! You get your hands off her!" I wasn't sure what Lance was planning to do about it if Jerry didn't listen, but when he started trying to sit up I realized that he was dead serious about doing something. In about two seconds, he was going to be out of that bed and all over Jerry and have himself and everything else messed up real good.

I laid a firm hand on his shoulder. "Hey, come on, take it easy," I said quietly, and got a poisonous look for my trouble. But he laid back, breathing hard, and I didn't know if I should give the credit to my firm hand or to the fact that he was still kind of short on blood and probably got dizzy if he tried to sit up too fast. Actually, he seemed to be having enough trouble keeping his head straight even without sitting up. Five minutes ago, he'd done everything but get right down to cussing Anne-Marie out himself. But just let Jerry try treating her the same way and, all of a sudden, it's a brand new ball game.

"It's all right, Lance," Anne-Marie said, pulling loose from Jerry's grasp with one irritated shrug. "Jerry was just leaving." She said it in the same tone you would use to send a muddy-footed dog out of the house.

Jerry glared around the room, looking like he wanted to punch everyone in sight. He opened his mouth to say something, met Anne-Marie's cold glare, and shut his mouth again. Then he turned and stalked off toward the door. He flung it open; then, as he went out, he came out with his most original and brilliant line yet. "You'll be sorry, Anne-Marie," he growled, and slammed the door behind him.

"I already am," Anne-Marie said softly, more to herself than to anyone else. I didn't know what she meant, but I was pretty sure it didn't have anything to do with ditching Jerry.

After all the yelling that had been going on there, the room suddenly seemed too quiet. As if everyone was too drained of emotion even to talk. Anne-Marie didn't try starting another conversation with Lance. I guess she was smart enough to know that defending her against Jerry and being ready to make peace with her were two different things.

"I'll get your clothes tomorrow, Lance," she said, sounding tired. "Red, I'll pick you up at your place at 1:00 and we'll go and sort them out."

I wanted to argue, refuse to go with her, tell her I was staying out of the whole deal, but I was just too tired to argue with her. Lance didn't say anything either and, without another word, Anne-Marie turned and walked out of the room.

There was a long silence after she left. I wondered what Lance was thinking — or, if he was like me, so tired and mixed-up that he wasn't really thinking at all. Finally I said, "I don't want to go with her to get your stuff. I don't want to do anything to make it easier for her — "

I wasn't finished but what Lance said stopped me. "Then do it to make it easier for *me*." His voice was low, his eyes steady on mine. After that, there weren't a whole lot of arguments left.

"What do you want to take with you?" I asked, fighting to keep my voice calm.

"I don't care," Lance said, and instantly my mind went back to the scene with Mr. Montrose that day. The words were the same, but there was one difference. This time I believed them. Lance didn't really care about much of anything now. "Just my clothes, I guess," he added, staring at the ceiling.

"What about all your art stuff?" I asked, thinking of the sketches that almost papered the walls of his bedroom. "You want your pencils and stuff, don't you?"

He shook his head. "No, you take it. I don't think I'll be using it any more." I stared at him, not believing he could mean it, and wondering if it was his hand he didn't think would ever be the same — or his heart. It seemed like he was leaving behind everything that mattered to him. Like in a war, when you know you have to surrender to the enemy, but first you make sure you've destroyed everything you have that they might want. That's what Lance was doing. Surrendering just a bombed-out shell of himself.

I didn't mean to say any more. It was his choice. His right to sort out his life any way that he wanted. It wasn't any of my business. But even as I was thinking that, I started saying the things that had been on my mind ever since he'd told me he was going with Anne-Marie. "It's not gonna work, Lance," I said. "I understand why you're doing it but it just isn't gonna work."

He turned to look at me. "Why not?"

"What you're doing is for your dad, right?"

He nodded and I went on. "You're keeping it out of court so your dad doesn't come out looking like some kind of a child beater or something, right?"

Another nod.

"So, what are you gonna do? Tell him that? Tell him that you're sacrificing yourself to keep him from looking bad?"

"No! He's never gonna know that's the reason. He can't find that out or he won't let me do it. Don't tell him, Red. Please," Lance said, panic rising in his voice. "Don't tell anybody."

"Okay, okay. Relax. I'm not gonna tell anyone. But you'd better think about what you're doing one more time. 'Cause, if you think that when you just up and tell him that, after all these years with him, you'd rather be with Anne-Marie, it's gonna make his day—"

"Quit it, Red!" Lance burst out, his voice shaking. "Don't you think I've thought about that? Do you think I want to do this? I'm doing it because I don't have any choice." He took a deep breath and went on, his voice quieter. "Well, about the same choice the vet gave me when Tomte's leg got smashed—cut it off or kill him. Some choice. And whatever I do now, Dad's gonna get hurt. The only choice I really get to make is how bad . . ." He tossed restlessly on the bed. "I just wish he'd get here so I could tell him and get it over with . . ." He stopped talking and just lay there, looking at me. It was my turn to say something. But there wasn't anything left for me to say.

I'm not sure how much later it was when the door opened and Dad and Mike walked in. I couldn't remember when I had ever been so glad to see my dad. Even though I knew better, I think that deep-down, I was half-expecting it to be like when I was real little. Whatever went wrong, Dad would sort it all out. He'd just walk into the room and make it all better . . .

I didn't remember getting up, but the next thing I knew, I was standing beside him. Neither of us said anything. Mike walked over to the bed and stood, looking silently down on Lance for a minute. "You okay?" he asked, at last.

Lance nodded. "Yeah," he said softly. "I'm okay, Dad." It should have been able to end there. Both of them glad to see each other. That quiet confidence they had in each other spreading calm through the room and healing all the wounds of the day.

But I knew that this time it couldn't end that way. I heard the change in Lance's voice as he said, "Dad, there's something I've got to tell you . . ."

And then I was walking out the door with Dad. It seemed like I'd somehow managed to get caught in the middle of every high-tension scene in this whole mess. But this time I wasn't staying. This was one scene I didn't think I could handle. I wasn't sure Lance could handle it either. But he didn't have a choice.

Dad and I walked down the hall to the little waiting area by the nurses' station and sat down to wait for Mike. At first, neither of us said anything. I couldn't say anything. All I could do was blink hard and stare into space. Even without looking in his direction, I could feel Dad watching me. Finally he said, "Red, are you all right?"

It's funny how automatic it is to answer "yes" to that question. I started to say it now, but it kind of got stuck in my throat. I shook my head and managed to get out a low "no." Dad came over and stood beside my chair. "What's the matter, Red? What's really going on, anyway?" he asked, his voice gentle.

I told him. I told him how Anne-Marie had left her big concert to come and see Lance. About how she and Jerry had split up over it. And about how Lance was going to go and live with Anne-Marie. The only thing I didn't tell him was the real reason why Lance was going. That was something I thought he'd be better off not knowing. It was something *I* would have been better off not knowing . . .

Dad looked bewildered. "Lance picked Anne-Marie over Mike. I never would have believed it," he said, mainly to himself. But the words wore on a raw spot in my mind. "Well, you better believe it," I snapped. " 'Cause it's the truth."

Dad gave me a funny look but he didn't say anything. He just walked over to the vending machine in the corner and fed in some coins. He came back carrying two cups of strong, black coffee. "Here," he said, handing one to me. "I think you can use this."

I took a big gulp. It burned my mouth but the bitterness tasted good. Just right for the mood I was in.

It wasn't much later when Mike came down the hall, walking slow, head down. Like he was real tired or real old. That was the first time I had ever noticed how much grey there was scattered through his dark hair. We stood up and Mike stopped in front of us. "He's goin' with her," he said, his voice flat and emotionless. His face looked blank, as if his own words hadn't really registered with him.

"You ready to go home, Mike?" Dad asked gently.

Mike nodded. "I've got nothin' to stay for," he said. Then, as he turned to walk toward the elevator, he added, "I guess she can give him a lot more than I can . . ." He couldn't hide the hurt in his voice now and I had to bite my tongue to keep from telling him . . .

Then I remembered my jacket still hanging on the chair in Lance's room. "Be right back, Dad," I said.

I burst into the room — and realized I should have knocked first. Lance was lying with his face buried in his pillow, crying. I wasn't surprised. What surprised me was that he had stayed in control for so long. But I figured that the scene with Mike just now must have been the worst of all. Especially since Lance hadn't even been able to tell him the truth. I doubted that Lance had ever held out on Mike before.

I felt guilty now for bursting in on Lance like that, but when he looked up at the sound of the door closing he didn't try to hide the tears.

I walked over and picked up my jacket. "I forgot my jacket," I said. Lance nodded. We looked at each other. I had to say something. Say what? Goodnight? Yeah, that would be real good. Have a good night, Lance. Have a great night. Spend it crying your guts out. See you the next time I'm passing through Nashville.

I didn't say goodnight. I thought of something else. A nice, big, stupid lie. "Hey," I said. "It's gonna be all right. Your dad'll get over it. He's okay . . ."

Even through the tears I could see the anger flare in Lance's eyes. "Stop it, Red! Stop tryin' to make me feel better. I don't want to feel better. I want it to hurt. I want it to hurt me as much as I hurt him . . ."

I stood there, feeling like an idiot. I just didn't know what to say. "Don't, Lance," I whispered. "It's not your fault."

"Just get outa here, Red. Get out and leave me alone."

"Sure," I said, my voice sounding choked. I could feel a big, hollow ache starting to grow in my chest. Was this it? The last chance I was going to get to say goodbye to my best friend and it ends like this? Blindly I reached for the door handle . . .

"Red?"

I turned back.

"Come back tomorrow."

The trip home was quiet. Quiet and fast. Dad had picked Mike up in the four-wheel-drive half-ton and they had come on to Calgary in it, but Dad drove that truck like it was a cop car — and he was in hot pursuit. I don't think there were twenty words exchanged in that cab from the moment we got in at the hospital until we pulled into Silverwinds an hour later.

Mike got out of the truck. "Thanks, Ken," he said. "Sorry to have been so much trouble." He stood there, unmoving, looking lost in his own backyard.

Dad got out and walked around the truck. "I'm sorry it had to turn out like this, Mike," was all he said. He laid his hand on Mike's shoulder for a second and then came back and got in.

I learned something about growing up then. Being

an adult doesn't make things a whole lot better, no matter what kids think. When your friend's hurting and there's nothing you can do to help, it isn't any easier to be forty than it is to be fifteen.

25

Dad let me stay home from school the next day — for a lot of reasons, I guess. It had been after one in the morning when we had finally got home and I hadn't slept much even after I got to bed. And even if I hadn't been so tired I could hardly see straight, there wouldn't have been much point in me going to school. I was too miserable to think about anything except Lance, anyway. And that led to the third reason why I had to stay home. Right after lunch, Anne-Marie was picking me up on her way to get Lance's stuff. I still didn't want to go with her. I didn't even want to see her again. But Lance had asked me to . . .

About one o'clock, a car pulled into the driveway. At first, I didn't know who it was. Just an ordinary Ford with rental plates . . . Then the door opened and Anne-Marie got out. I guessed the Lincoln must have been one of the fringe-benefits that had disappeared when Jerry had — but I figured that the exchange had still been worth it.

She wasn't feeling very talkative and I was glad, since "Hello" was more than I felt like saying to her. We drove over to Silverwinds in silence. Mike's truck was nowhere in sight so I figured that Lance had set it all up this way. Given Mike the chance to be away when Anne-Marie came.

The back seat of the Ford was full of empty suitcases. Expensive ones. Nothing but the best, I thought sourly. We each took a couple and headed into the house. The door wasn't locked. It never was. Mike wasn't the door-locking kind.

Anne-Marie wandered through the living room, looking around, picking up a book or an ornament, turning it around in her hands, putting it down again. I wondered what kind of memories this house held for her. I just hoped that, whatever they were, they hurt. I hoped they hurt real bad.

I turned and went into Lance's room. Nothing had changed much since the last time I'd been here, before Lance had got mad at me. But today when I looked around, I noticed everything like I was seeing it for the first time. Maybe it was because, as far as I could figure it, I was probably seeing it for the last time.

The room was semi-messy. Not so bad that stuff reached out and tried to grab your ankles when you walked through — mine has been known to be that bad. But this was kid-comfortable. Everything was handy, not stuffed away in some drawer where he might forget he had it. One lone sock, lying on the dresser, waiting hopefully for the return of its long-lost mate. Half a bag of taco chips on the floor within convenient reach of the bed for emergency late-night energy. A pair of spurs, dangling by their chains from the closet door. A half-read western paperback sticking out from under the bed. The ghetto-blaster that Mike had given Lance for Christmas, sitting on the desk with a pile of tapes beside it, including one tape dead but as yet unburied, its plastic entrails hanging in long, slinky ribbons over the edge of the desk. Bobbi-Jo Carson's school picture stuck in the corner of the mirror — I hadn't noticed that before but it didn't come as too big a surprise . . .

And all over the rest of his desk, art stuff — the things I was supposed to have but that I knew I couldn't make myself take. Pencils, erasers, charcoal, felts, pencil crayons, a few tubes of oil paint . . . And, everywhere, his pictures. Not framed or even finished up most of the time, mainly just sheets ripped out of his sketch pad and tacked to the wall. Pencil sketches of animals — deer, wolves, horses, Tomte looking so real he practically purred . . . But one thing was missing. The eagle picture. For a minute, I was afraid maybe he had thrown it away. Then, under a pile of schoolbooks on the dresser, I saw it, covered up except for one corner. I walked over and stood, looking down at it. I didn't want the drawing stuff. I could never do the kind of things with it that Lance did. But if he was going to give me something, I didn't think he'd mind if I took the picture. I reached down, started to move the books. I noticed some lettering at the top of the paper. That fantastic three-dimensional stuff that Lance made look easy. He had finished the picture up as a poster. IF — that was the first word. I lifted the books.

But, as I did, I heard a footstep behind me. I set them back down and turned around, feeling almost guilty. It was Anne-Marie, of course. She didn't say anything. Just stood there, looking around, her face as beautiful as ever but different somehow. Kind of haunted . . .

I realized that I couldn't do what Lance had asked. I couldn't sit here, in his room, going through his stuff, with this stranger who had just walked in and destroyed his life. Even being here without him was bad enough. It made me feel as if he was dead. I knew that if I didn't get out of here I was going to start bawling. I didn't look at Anne-Marie. I turned and walked toward door. "I'll wait out here," I said, my voice going kind of rough.

She didn't answer so I went on out to the kitchen and walked around, looking at things and not really seeing them. Saying goodbye.

Tomte was lying on the table, singing to himself and looking smug. He gave one of his little "murrps" that Lance always said mean "hello," when he saw me standing there, I picked him up, holding him the way he likes to be carried, thrown across your shoulder like a baby about to be burped. "And you can quit that sleeping-on-the-table-routine, right now," I told him. " 'Cause, from now on, Lance won't be around to stick up for you and spoil you rotten. Things are gonna be different around here — a whole lot different . . ." My voice went funny on me and I smothered a sob in Tomte's thick fur. I wished Anne-Marie would hurry up. I couldn't take much more of this.

It seemed a long time later when she finally walked into the kitchen. "Let's go, Red," was all she had to say, and her voice sounded strange, sort of soft and rough, all at the same time. She stood looking out the window and I couldn't see her face.

"I'll get the suitcases," I said.

She shook her head, "No, this is all I'm taking." I looked around. All I could see was a big, brown bag and a rolled-up paper with an elastic around it. My mind went back to the story she had told me about the day she had run away with Mike. "We went by my house and got my stuff. It filled two grocery bags . . ." And now it seemed like she was only allowing Lance one. She probably figured his old stuff wasn't good enough, anyhow. She could buy him better — buy him anything he wanted. Except for the one thing he really wanted. She couldn't buy him that.

She had turned and was walking toward the door

when I suddenly realized how much I really did want to have that picture. "Just a minute," I said. "I'll be right out." I ran back to Lance's room and started to pick up the pile of books on his dresser. But I put them back again. It was gone. The eagle picture was gone. I remembered the rolled-up paper in Anne-Marie's hand and I hated her. I hated her a lot. Taking my best friend wasn't enough for her. Now she'd even taken my picture.

I got in the car and slammed the door, hard. I wouldn't look at Anne-Marie but I could feel her taking a long look at me. She didn't say anything. She just pulled out onto the road and headed straight for Calgary. She didn't even ask me if I wanted to come to the hospital with her — which I didn't. But I knew I had to. Tomorrow Lance would be out of the hospital — and out of my life. Today was goodbye.

All the way to the city it was quiet in that car, just as quiet as the trip home had been last night. Anne-Marie's mind seemed to be a long way off. So far away I wasn't sure she even remembered that I was with her. That was fine with me because I sure didn't feel like talking. I wished she'd keep her mind on her driving, though. It had started to rain and the pavement was plenty slippery for her not to notice red lights until she was already into the intersection. By the time we got to the hospital, my nerves were shot. Looking back on it now, that trip in Randy's Corvette didn't seem so scary in comparison to riding with Anne-Marie.

She pulled into a parking space and I started to open the door but she stopped me. "Red," she said, her voice hesitant, as though she knew she was on dangerous ground. "You've always been good at being honest with me. Try it one more time. Why did Lance give in and decide to come with me without the custody case even going to court?"

I looked at her. I looked at her for a long time while

the two halves of my mind fought each other for the answer. "Tell her," one part said. "Tell her the only reason he's willing to leave Mike is because he loves him too much to see him hurt. Tell her and maybe it'll make a difference—just maybe she'll turn around and go back to Nashville."

"Don't you dare tell her," the other half said. "Lance would die before he'd let anyone find out the reason behind what he's doing. And you promised him. You owe him. He probably saved your life. Keeping your word to him is the least you can do."

Finally I sighed and shook my head. "I can't answer that question," I said. "If you want to know so bad, ask Lance."

Anne-Marie gave a little laugh. "And do you think he's likely to tell me?"

"No," I admitted.

"But it isn't because he feels any different than he ever did about being with me, is it Red?" she asked, her eyes demanding an answer. "He still hates the idea, doesn't he?"

I met her look. "He doesn't want to go," I said.

She nodded. "Thanks," she said, but I didn't know why she should be grateful for that answer.

We walked into the hospital in silence. Just inside the door she stopped and turned to face me. Suddenly it struck me how uncertain she looked. I didn't see why. She had won the battle. All she had to do now was claim the trophy and ride away into the sunset.

"Red," she said in a low voice, "I'd like to talk to Lance alone. Do you mind waiting awhile?"

Since when did what I did or didn't mind matter to her? I shrugged. "I'll wait," I said, and watched as she walked away. I thought of how hard Lance had always fought to keep from having to be alone with Anne-Marie. If he knew I had let her get rid of me this easy, he'd be mad. But he was going to have to get used to the idea of it being just the two of them. That was the way it was going to be from now on . . .

I felt a big lump settling in my throat. I didn't like having to wait here alone. It was too easy to start thinking . . .

I had to wait a long time. I wondered what Lance and Anne-Marie could find to talk about for that long. It seemed like all their conversations so far had been no-holds-barred fights.

Finally I went over to the vending machine and bought a Coke. I was just turning around with it in my hand when I saw her come in. But she didn't see me at first. Or, if she did, I don't think me being there actually registered with her. She just kept on walking right across the room, her head high and her eyes focused somewhere in the distance. She didn't have the grocery bag any more but the rolled-up paper was still in her hand.

She stopped by the window and stood looking out at the parking lot. I walked up behind her and waited for her to turn around and see me standing there, but she didn't. She just kept staring at the parking lot like it was one of the Seven Wonders of the World. I was running out of time. Dad was coming to pick me up in less than an hour. That wasn't much time. I wanted to spend it with Lance.

"What's the matter?" I asked at last, my voice sounding loud in the silence. She still didn't answer me but she half-turned toward me and I understood why she couldn't answer. She was crying. She cried the same way she did everything else — with a lot of pride and class. She didn't make a sound. Just stood there with her head high and the tears silently sliding down her cheeks. Without a word, she handed me the paper. I looked at it blankly and then back to her for some clue. But she was staring out into the rain again.

Slowly I started to unroll the paper. I didn't know why I needed to. I was already sure it was the eagle picture — the picture I'd first seen the same night that I'd first seen Anne-Marie. It had been raining then, too, that Friday night when she had walked across a TV screen and back into her son's life.

I was right. It was the picture. And it was even better than I had remembered it. The eagle could have been a photograph, it was so real, so perfect. But it was better than a photograph. No camera could ever catch the feeling, the freedom and wild defiance the way Lance had.

Then I unrolled it a little farther and read the words that Lance had added:

IF YOU LOVE SOMETHING, LET IT GO

At first the words didn't mean anything that special. I'd seen them on posters before. They were part of a longer quotation but I couldn't think of the rest of it right now. They had always made me think of wild animals locked up in cages. People holding onto things that had a right to be free . . .

Then, as I thought those last words, the meaning of it all hit me like a fist in the stomach. The poster said everything that Lance would have told Anne-Marie if he hadn't been too proud and too tore-up to say it. She wanted him because she loved him. But, if she loved him enough, she could never have him . . .

Now I understood why she was crying.

The score was tied, one to one. Now they had both made each other cry. If this was love, I thought hate would hurt a lot less.

I looked up at Anne-Marie and this time she was looking at me. She had stopped crying and was back in control again. Herself again. But not quite the same as she had been before. I didn't think Anne-Marie would ever be quite the same again. But she'd be a whole lot better. Maybe now she could understand Lance a little more. Give him a chance to see the good side of her. Stop trying so hard not to love her. I still couldn't stand the thought of him having to leave here, but maybe, just maybe, he could survive with her now . . .

I started to roll up the poster but something in the bottom corner caught my eye. More printing. Smaller. Neat. But stiff and backward slanting. The sort of printing a right-handed person would do if they had to use their left hand . . .

THANKS FOR LOVING ME THAT MUCH, MOM.

I think I forgot to breathe for a few seconds. I stood, frozen, looking up at Anne-Marie, searching her face for answers that I was afraid I wouldn't get. Wondering if I could possibly be reading the right meaning into those words.

Anne-Marie smiled, a kind of shaky smile that looked like it might dissolve on her if she let her guard down. "I brought him some clean clothes to wear home," she said. "The nurse says Mike can pick him up anytime after noon tomorrow."

Now all the pieces were falling into place. The grocery bag. She'd only brought one set of clothes because she knew she wouldn't be taking Lance with her . . .

I wondered when she had made up her mind. From the moment she had first seen the poster? Even before that? But it didn't really matter when she had decided. All that mattered was the choice that she had made. Without even thinking what I was doing, I threw my arms around her. And she hugged me back, hard. And then I realized that I was crying, too. But it didn't hurt at all. I felt great. I didn't even care that everyone in the waiting room was staring at us. Let them stare. Let them eat their hearts out. It wasn't every red-headed, fifteen-year-old who got hugged by Anne-Marie Charbonneau . . .

Then she was putting her coat on. I handed her the poster and she put it inside her coat where it wouldn't get wet. "Well, Red," she said. "I'm glad I met you. Come down to Nashville and visit sometime. And stay honest. I like you that way." Then she turned and walked away, fast. She didn't look back.

I watched her disappear into the rain. And I wondered if she'd be okay. I wondered how much damage she had done to her career by skipping that concert. And how much of Jerry's threat could he back up? But then I thought about how far Anne-Marie had come from that northern Saskatchewan shack and I knew that, in spite of everything, she'd make it. She was a survivor. Just like Lance. And Lance would make it, too. That cut wouldn't stop him. He'd be back drawing again, if he wanted to bad enough. And I was pretty sure he was going to want to . . .

They'd both make it.

And suddenly I remembered the rest of that quotation even though I wasn't sure of the exact words: "If you love something, let it go. If it comes back to you, it's yours. If it doesn't, it never was."

Anne-Marie might be going away again. She and Lance would be a thousand miles apart. But they had already come a long way back to each other. One of these days I was going to accept that invitation to visit Nashville. And I didn't think I'd be going alone . . .

Epilogue

I went with Mike to the hospital the next day. While he was signing a bunch of papers at the desk I went to get Lance. He was just getting dressed when I got to his room.

"Hey, Paleface! It's about time you got here," he said, fastening his belt with his good hand and flashing that old, challenging grin. "What took you so long, anyhow?"

I shrugged. "Without my Corvette, what can you expect?" I said. "And," I added disgustedly, "my dad made me go to school for morning classes so I didn't miss math."

Lance laughed. "He hasn't changed," he said.

Yeah, I thought. Dad has changed. Or I have. Maybe both of us. But I wasn't ready to try to explain that yet. Not even to Lance. Anyway, he wasn't listening any more.

"Let's get out of this place," he said. "Grab my shirt out of the cupboard, will ya?" I walked over and got it. He pulled off his pajama top and turned to take the shirt from me. And as he did, a flash of gold against his chest caught my eye.

The St. Christopher's Medal.

I must have been standing there gaping at it like a fish out of water because Lance looked down at it for a second too. Then his eyes met mine. "My mom got it fixed for me," he said softly.

Have you seen
the Hardy Boys
lately?

Now you can continue to enjoy the Hardy Boys in a new action-packed series written especially for older readers. Each book has more high-tech adventure, intrigue, mystery and danger than ever before.

Join Frank and Joe in these fabulous adventures, available only in Armada.

1	Dead on Target	£2.25	☐
2	Evil, Incorporated	£2.25	☐
3	Cult of Crime	£2.25	☐
4	The Lazarus Plot	£2.25	☐

ARMADA

The Hardy Boys Mystery Stories

ARMADA

The Three Investigators
Series

Meet the Three Investigators – brilliant Jupiter Jones, athletic Pete Crenshaw and studious Bob Andrews. Their motto, "We investigate anything" has led them into some bizarre and dangerous situations. Join the three boys in their sensational mysteries, available only in Armada.

ARMADA

The Pit

ANN CHEETHAM

The summer has hardly begun when Oliver Wright is plunged into a terrifying darkness. Gripped by fear when workman Ted Hoskins is reduced to a quivering child at a demolition site, Oliver believes something of immense power has been disturbed. But what?

Caught between two worlds – the confused present and the tragic past – Oliver is forced to let events take over.

£1.95 ☐

Nightmare Park

LINDA HOY

A highly original and atmospheric thriller set around a huge modern theme park, a theme park where teenagers suddenly start to disappear . . .

£1.95 ☐

ARMADA

Run With the Hare

LINDA NEWBERY

A sensitive and authentic novel exploring the workings of an animal rights group, through the eyes of Elaine, a sixth-form pupil. Elaine becomes involved with the group through her more forceful friend Kate, and soon becomes involved with Mark, an Adult Education student and one of the more sophisticated members of the group. Elaine finds herself painting slogans and sabotaging a fox hunt. Then she and her friends uncover a dog fighting ring – and things turn very nasty.

£1.95 ☐

Hairline Cracks

JOHN ROBERT TAYLOR

A gritty, tense and fast-paced story of kidnapping, fraud and cover ups. Sam Lydney's mother knows too much. She's realized that a public inquiry into the safety of a nuclear power station has been rigged. Now she's disappeared and Sam's sure she has been kidnapped, he can trust no one except his resourceful friend Mo, and together they are determined to uncover the crooks' operation and, more importantly, find Sam's mother.

£1.95 ☐

ARMADA

All these books are available at your local bookshop or newsagent, or can be ordered from the publisher. To order direct from the publishers just tick the title you want and fill in the form below:

Name _____

Address _____

_____

Send to: Collins Childrens Cash Sales
          PO Box 11
          Falmouth
          Cornwall
          TR10 9EN

Please enclose a cheque or postal order or debit my Visa/ Access –

   Credit card no:

   Expiry date:

   Signature:

– to the value of the cover price plus:

UK: 60p for the first book, 25p for the second book, plus 15p per copy for each additional book ordered to a maximum charge of £1.90.

BFPO: 60p for the first book, 25p for the second book plus 15p per copy for the next 7 books, thereafter 9p per book.

Overseas and Eire: £1.25 for the first book, 75p for the second book. Thereafter 28p per book.

Armada reserve the right to show new retail prices on covers which may differ from those previously advertised in the text or elswhere.

ARMADA